MW01128168

The Giant Horseshoe Mystery

George S. Haines

authorHOUSE®

AuthorHouse™
1663 Liberty Drive, Suite 200
Bloomington, IN 47403
www.authorhouse.com
Phone: 1-800-839-8640

First published by AuthorHouse 4/14/2008

ISBN: 978-1-4343-4099-3 (sc)
ISBN: 978-1-4343-6151-6 (hc)

Library of Congress Control Number: 2007907394

Printed in the United States of America
Bloomington, Indiana

This book is printed on acid-free paper.

Coming Soon:
Another Sam And Howie Adventure
Adventure

The X Y Z Mystery

THIS BOOK IS DEDICATED TO THE MEMORY OF MY WIFE, BONITA, WHO ALWAYS GAVE ME INSPIRATION AND ENCOURAGEMENT. I AM IN GRATITUDE TO MY DAUGHTERS, PAMELA AND GEORGANA, FOR THEIR PRAYERS AND CONTINUOUS SUPPORT. ALWAYS IN MY PRAYERS ARE MY THREE GRANDCHILDREN, JUSTIN, KAYLE AND MATTHEW, WHO ARE DESTINED TO BE OF SERVICE TO GOD AND MANKIND.

ALSO, I AM INDEBTED TO JANNET McCOLLUM, RUSS KRAAY, ERWIN RUDOLPH, STEPHANIE BEAM, AND LOU GERIG FOR THEIR SUGGESTIONS.

SPECIAL THANKS TO BETTY WEDELES FOR HER ARTISTIC INSIGHTS AND TALENTS IN THE CREATION AND DEVELOPMENT OF ALL COVER AND INSIDE IMAGES

THE GIANT HORSESHOE MYSTERY

Sam, age 11, is an eager explorer around the farm where he lives in rural Indiana during the 1930's. His cousin Howie, age 10, comes for a relaxing visit. This visit, however, soon turns into a hair-raising adventure as Sam and Howie embark on some exploring adventures and discover some long-hidden secrets.

Together they explore an abandoned log cabin on the farm and make a gruesome discovery…..a skeleton in an underground tunnel. And, the skeleton is holding a large piece of metal in the shape of a horseshoe.

Is the skeleton the result of a murder? Why is the skeleton holding the giant horseshoe? Are there clues hidden on the horseshoe that will help answer these and other questions?

Sam and Howie soon find out that they are not the only persons seeking a solution to this mystery. Two strange men continually threaten and harass them. Why do these men want the horseshoe? Do they think it might provide clues that will lead to something valuable?

Will Sam and Howie find the solution to this mystery before the strange men do? Follow along as Sam and Howie are determined to be the first to follow the clues and find the solution to the mystery of the giant horseshoe.

TO COUSIN HOWIE

As you know, I am young and not so wise at all,
That sometimes I may succeed, but many times I fall.

But to explore and discover is all I want to do,
The events that are past: the what, the why, and the who.

What we just imagine may take over and run wild,
But the secrets it discovers may make our thoughts seem mild.

Just to know what is in the running stream or in the pond,
And all that is around them, under, and beyond.

The fields and trees have interest of what used to be,
And beckon us to visit and take time to see.

The grand old log cabin and the nearby unused barn,
Have regions to visit and listen for an oft-told yarn.

All of the old buildings have a dignity and charm that is past,
But the character they lived, gives us memories that will last.

When we go exploring, be prepared to find,
A mystery that goes well beyond the borders of our mind.

We could even find a mystery that may our wits defy,
And make us ask some questions, like what, who, and why?

But in the end, whether or not the mystery is solved,
You will agree for sure it was exciting to be involved.

FROM YOUR COUSIN SAM

Contents

CHAPTER 1 A CLOSE CALL 9
CHAPTER 2 HOWIE COMES FOR A VISIT 13
CHAPTER 3 QUEENIE FALLS IN THE WELL 19
CHAPTER 4 SAM'S IMAGINATION 25
CHAPTER 5 EXPLORING THE LOG CABIN 31
CHAPTER 6 THE SKELETON 37
CHAPTER 7 THE GIANT HORSESHOE 41
CHAPTER 8 THE CLUES 49
CHAPTER 9 SHERIFF NEVERFINE INVESTIGATES 57
CHAPTER 10 TWO STRANGE MEN 65
CHAPTER 11 THE STONE FIREPLACE WALL 69
CHAPTER 12 THE UNDERGROUND RAILROAD 75
CHAPTER 13 SAM AND HOWIE IN JAIL 87
CHAPTER 14 WHAT DO THE CLUES MEAN? 95
CHAPTER 15 SLY AND SLICK 101
CHAPTER 16 THE COPPER BOX 105
CHAPTER 17 THE CONTENTS REVEALED 109
CHAPTER 18 THE ROYAL STAR 115
CHAPTER 19 SLY AND SLICK IN JAIL 123
CHAPTER 20 PUFF: THE REST OF THE STORY 127
CHAPTER 21 THE MYSTERY SOLVED 133

LOOK OUT, MARY

CHAPTER 1

A CLOSE CALL

A loud, deep bellowing sound of an engine brought Sam to his senses. He looked to his right and saw a black car roaring toward them at a terrific rate of speed. Alarm bells went off in his head. Mary, his sister, was in the middle of the road, her eyes and mind focused on the cows grazing in a field beyond.

Sam acted without thinking. He rushed forward, grabbed Mary by the waist and pushed her into the ditch at the far side of the road. The car thundered by just as they landed headlong in the knee-high grass. Sam glanced up and saw two men in the speeding black car. He got a good look at the man on the passenger side. His long red hair was flowing in the wind.

As the car quickly disappeared in the distance, Sam and Mary picked themselves up and brushed the dirt and dust from their clothes.

"Are you hurt, Mary?" asked Sam, still out of breath.

"A little shook up," she replied, as she stood up. She straightened her grass-stained dress and smoothed back her hair. "I'll get the mail; then, let's get back to the house and tell mom what happened!"

It was a hot, peaceful July morning on the farmstead owned by Wilmer and Millie in North Central Indiana. Their place was called "The HayBend Farm," named after Wilmer's grandparents. Record breaking high temperatures and the lack of rain were causing the corn and other crops to wilt. The dry weather in the western states was turning the soil into dust. That dust, blowing eastward, was visible for miles in the air over the HayBend farmstead. Sometimes it was difficult to see the barn from the house, a distance of only a few hundred feet. The severe weather of the 1930's was causing suffering to the people and damage to the land they depended on to scratch out a living.

A gentle breeze stirred the leaves on five large maple shade trees that framed the farmhouse where Wilmer and Millie lived with their daughter, Mary, and their son, Sam. Sidney, the mailman, driving his dust covered Oldsmobile, had just dropped off the mail at the end of a long lane leading from the house to the road. Sidney was a small wiry man. He had a long moustache that curved up on the ends and jiggled up and down when he laughed. He had been a rural mail carrier for years. His Oldsmobile had carried him and the mail through snow, ice, rain, fog and sunshine. He considered country folks his family, and he knew they looked forward to the daily newspaper and letters he brought them. He was a popular man, and he knew Sam and Mary by name.

Mary and Sam had walked slowly down the long lane that connected their farmstead to the road. The hot humid days of summer seemed to slow everybody down. They wanted to pick up the daily newspaper, called the GrantNews, and any letters or postcards that Sidney might have left in the mailbox.

The lane consisted of two strips of gravel separated by a grassy ridge. Wilted corn plants, showing the effects of the dry weather, were growing in a field on one side of the lane. On the other side pigs in a pasture were squealing and fighting for the limited shade provided by a few trees along the fence.

Sam wore a tattered, sweat-stained straw hat, faded and patched bib overalls, a blue shirt and hi-top work shoes. Mary's dress was of thin plain cotton and her scuffed brown shoes were topped off with a pair of soiled white anklets.

Mary was three years older and could walk a little faster so she had reached the end of the lane first. Sam was always a few steps behind because he had the habit of kicking his shoes in the gravel and daydreaming. With his hands in his pockets and his head down, he was lost in his thoughts about his actual and imagined adventures exploring the land and buildings around the farm.

Mary started to cross the road to reach the mailbox on the other side. She did not expect to see any cars as the concrete road was used by only a few motorists. The cows on the other side of the road greeted her with loud "moos". She did not see or hear the black car bearing down upon her. It was at that moment Sam realized Mary was in grave danger, and rushed to push her out of harm's way.

As they hurried back to the house, they looked through the mail. The only item other than the GrantNews was a letter from their Aunt Lenora, Uncle Francis and Cousin Howie. They lived in the neighboring state of Ohio, about a three-hour drive from the HayBend Farm.

Sam held the envelope up to the sun but still couldn't see what was inside. "We'll ask mom to read it to us," he said, as they started to run back to the farmhouse.

He added, between breaths, "I hope cousin Howie is coming. We haven't been exploring around the farm for a long time."

The farmhouse was a large, two-story home, built 50 years ago. A green shingle roof topped off the well-kept home. The wood siding was painted white. Green shutters decorated each side of the numerous windows.

As Sam and Mary entered the kitchen, they found their father, Wilmer, and mother, Millie, sitting at the dining table enjoying a glass of cold lemonade. They were discussing the hot weather and its effect on the corn crop. They were very worried that the crop would be a failure because of the lack of rain. The kitchen was quite simple, with a sink, large cupboard, small refrigerator, kerosene cooking stove, and wooden dining table with four chairs. A seven-day wind up clock hung from a nail driven into the wall above the cooking stove. Below the clock hung a framed passage from Psalm 66; verses 1-2 including these words: 'Tell everyone on this earth to shout praises to God. Sing about his glorious name. Honor him with praises.' Millie had reworded the verses from the King James Version of the Bible and put them in a frame when she was 10 years old.

Wilmer had been working in the barn and his long-sleeved, blue shirt was soaked with perspiration. He was not a tall man, probably five feet, seven inches in height, but very muscular and strong. Millie was about the same height but heavier. Her grey hair was always combed back to form a bun at the back of her head.

"Did you get the paper, Sam?" asked Wilmer.

"Yep, here it is," he responded, as he handed the newspaper to his father. "But, dad, first we need to tell you and mom what happened when Mary crossed the road to pick up the mail!" urged Sam, his voice rising.

Both Wilmer and Millie could tell that Sam was serious. They sat back and listened quietly as Sam and Mary told them how a speeding black car almost ran over Mary as she was crossing the road.

"Mary, are you hurt in any way?" asked her mother.

"No," she responded, "just a little sore. I'll be alright."

"And, there were two men in the car; one had red hair!" added Sam, with excitement. "That car was the only car on the road. Why were those men in such a hurry?"

"I really don't know," Wilmer mused, as he unfolded the newspaper. "You did a very brave thing, son. We're proud of you."

"It's a good thing you were there and saw that car coming, Sam," said Millie, as she put her arm around Mary and gave her a hug. "You probably saved your sister from serious injury. Mary, why don't you go upstairs and put on a clean dress?" she continued.

Sam took off his straw hat, sat down at the table and poured himself a glass of ice cold lemonade. He rubbed his hands around the glass and then across his forehead trying to cool off. He began to relax and think back about what had just happened. As he slowly drained his glass, he was thinking out loud, "The only car on the road, going very fast, out here in the country. Why? Why?"

It was difficult for him to erase from his mind the picture of his sister Mary lying in the grass at the side of the road beside him, the blur of the black car racing by, and the passenger with the long, flowing red hair, laughing at them as he passed by. Sam said to himself, "I hope we never see those two men again."

CHAPTER 2

HOWIE COMES FOR A VISIT

"Oh, I almost forgot, this letter came today," Sam said, as he handed the envelope to his mother. "It's from Uncle Francis and Aunt Lenora, mom."

Millie wiped her brow and hands on her well-worn apron that was frayed around the edges. Across the front of the apron the words 'God Bless Our Home' were printed in large green letters. Faded food spots of various colors were proof of many past days of working in the kitchen. She reached for the letter opener, slit the top open, and began to read.

"Oh," she said. "Oh my gracious, they are coming for a visit next week. Oh! I will need to lay in some groceries and clean the entire house. Oh… next week."

She furrowed her brow and firmed up her lips as she finished reading. She then handed the letter to Wilmer. She was never happy when Wilmer's sister Lenora, Uncle Francis and Howie came to visit. Millie felt that Lenora, who was born and reared on a farm, was always judging her ability to be a "good farm wife."

When Wilmer and Millie were married and started housekeeping a few years ago, they had no inside plumbing, no electricity, no telephone, no running water in the house and no close neighbors. In the nearby town of Manion, where Millie grew up, she had all of these advantages.

Wilmer had been busy reading the front page news. He looked up at Millie and said, "A robbery has been reported at one of our neighbor's homes. The Katchnot's house, down the road west a mile, was broken into yesterday."

"Oh! Why, I was talking to Sadie Katchnot just last week. We were both at the ladies meeting at the church," Millie said, alarmed. "Was she hurt in any way?"

"No," responded Wilmer, "they were in town buying groceries when the robbery occurred. According to the report, the police found some footprints on a dusty path back of the house. They think that there were two robbers involved. They stole jewelry and some old gold coins. They left the house in a mess."

Sam, who had been listening closely, broke in. "Gee, dad, two robbers that close to our farm. We need to keep the shotgun handy."

Wilmer, with a frown, turned to look at Sam, and then ignoring him, continued reading. "The Katchnot's neighbor, who lives across the road from them, recalled seeing two men in an old black car parked nearby on the side of the road. One had red hair and the other had dark hair. The sheriff has no other leads in the case."

When Sam heard the words red hair, his ears immediately perked up. "Hey, wait a minute, dad. Do you suppose the men in the car that almost ran over Mary this morning are the same men as those mentioned in the newspaper?"

"Hmmm...I think it's possible, son," responded Wilmer, as he turned to face Millie. "This robbery is rather worrisome, being that close to our farm."

"Yes, it is," replied Millie, with a worried look on her face. "We need to keep our eyes open."

* * * *

The days passed quickly and Uncle Francis and his family arrived on schedule in the late afternoon, driving a late model, shiny, green Chevrolet. After the usual greetings, handshakes and smiles, they lifted their suitcases out of the trunk of the car and brought them into the house. The two families didn't do much hugging. Sam and Howie were taught not to show affection in public. Sam had never seen his father and mother hug each other.

Sam and Howie looked at each other and nodded. Howie, with his shirt tail hanging out, looked rumpled and tired. He carried his small, yellow and red plaid suitcase upstairs to Sam's bedroom, a room simply furnished with a bed, chest of drawers, bookcase, and a small clothes closet. They sat on the edge of the bed and looked quietly at their shoes for a few minutes. Then Sam opened up and asked Howie, "Have you explored around your farm since the last visit?"

Howie thought for a few seconds, and then said, "No, not much, Sam. You know I'm not much of an explorer."

"Well," Sam responded, "we're going to explore while you're here this time. I've got some exciting ideas!"

Wilmer and his family visited back and forth with Uncle Francis and his family two or three times a year. Aunt Lenora, Wilmer's older sister, had married Francis late in life and Howie was their only child. He was a year younger than Sam, and a little shorter in height, so naturally Sam thought he should be the leader when they went exploring around the farm. Uncle Francis did not encourage Howie to be an outdoors boy. However, when Howie came to visit, he reluctantly joined Sam in his exploring ventures.

Cousin Howie was usually quieter than Sam. When he was around Francis, his dad, he could not squeeze a word in. Sam and Howie were taught never to interrupt an adult when that person was talking.

However, when Howie and Sam were together they forgot about the differences in their families. They enjoyed being with each other and exploring around the farm. Since no other boys Sam's age lived close by, he looked forward to Howie's visits. Then he could stretch his imagination to the limit as he planned their exploring adventures.

After an hour or so of talking about what had happened since the last visit, they were restless. Sam took out his pocket watch and said, "Come on, Howie, let's go outdoors and play ball. We've got an hour before supper."

"Okay. When did you get that pocket watch, Sam? That's a nice one."

"Yeah, mom and dad got it for me last Christmas. See, it fits in this little pocket on the front of my overalls."

They picked up a softball and a bat from the floor of the clothes closet and headed outside to hit the ball to each other, and to play catch. Howie did not have much experience playing ball but he got a lot of exercise chasing the ball around the barnyard.

Finally, Millie appeared at the door to the back porch of the house. "Boys, come in now. Supper will be ready in 15 minutes."

"Whew! I'm glad. It's hot out here," said Howie, with relief. "Come on, Sam, let's get in there. I'm hungry."

* * * *

That evening at the supper table Sam and Howie listened to the adults talk about politics, the dry weather and the wilting corn and other crops. After eating their fill, they went up to Sam's room to look at some old Batman comic books.

Although both Sam and Howie lived on farms, they had different responsibilities. Howie helped with some of the farm chores in and around the barn. Sam worked from dawn to dusk doing all kinds of farm work. This included preparing the soil, planting and tending the crops.

Wilmer let Sam drive the team of horses, the farm tractor and the old truck around the barnyard and fields. He had chores to do before and after school. Because of the "hands-on" work, Sam and Wilmer were called "dirt farmers" by their relatives who lived in the city. They worked the soil and usually had a collection of dirt under their fingernails.

Uncle Francis was a "gentleman farmer." He was never seen in dirty work clothes. He always wore a tie with his long-sleeved shirt. His pants were held up with red suspenders. A straw hat completed his summer outfit. He had a pleasant personality and was always talking, and, as a result, he was a very successful salesman.

Howie looked at the comic books for over an hour. Then, rather bored, he asked, "Sam, what are we going to do tomorrow?"

"Howie, I've planned some exciting adventures while you're here.

We're going to explore around the farm."

Howie thought for a while. Then he said, "I hope you're not going to take me down the road to that old gravel pit again, the one that's full of water. We never did catch any fish, and that inner tube I was floating on sprung a leak and I had to swim to shore. That was scary. Then, the last time I was here that big hog chased me clear across the pasture field. When I jumped the fence she was right on my tail."

"No, Howie, we are not going to the gravel pit; and, we'll stay out of the hog lots. It was your own fault the hog chased you. I told you not to go out in that field where the mother hog and the little pigs were. She was protecting her young.

This time we are going to see some real excitement. I've decided we need a real challenge, a challenge to discover something. We can explore and discover right here on this farm. Then, we can go across the road and explore on Grandpa George's farm. Are you with me, Howie?"

"Yeah, Sam, I'm with you. Just don't make it too exciting."

Sam had already read the tattered comic books several times. He was holding one in his lap but he wasn't looking at the pages. His mind was elsewhere. He was planning their adventures for the next several days.

CHAPTER 3

QUEENIE FALLS IN THE WELL

The next day after the noon meal Sam took Howie aside and said, "Today we're going to explore the woods at the back of the farm. I want to show you some animals you haven't seen before."

"Okay, Sam, that doesn't sound too scary. How big are the animals?"

Sam ignored the question. After all, he thought, they weren't going to the zoo.

The woods had large trees, dense brush and undergrowth that made good hiding places for large, wild animals. The remains of old rail fences on three sides of the woods provided good cover for nesting birds.

Wilmer did not need the horses for work that day so Sam put a bridle on Queenie and led her to the watering tank. He rubbed her neck as she drank her fill. He and Howie could then stand on the edge of the tank and swing one leg over her back to get astride. Sam held the reins with one hand and grabbed Queenie's mane with the other hand and pulled himself over on to her back. He then held on to Howie's arm and helped him up behind.

As they rode away from the large, red barn toward the distant woods, Howie asked, "Sam, are you sure it's safe to ride this old flea bag?"

"Sure, I've been riding Queenie for years. She's old and very tame. And, she's not an old flea bag."

They both rode bareback because Wilmer did not own a saddle for Queenie. Sam was in front with Howie hanging on to the back straps of Sam's bib overalls for support. Queenie, a gentle work horse, was very wide across her back. Howie and Sam felt that their legs would come unhinged. Her large body swayed back and forth as she slowly walked the narrow path that led to the woods.

"Sam, my legs are sticking straight out. Are all horses this fat?"

"Howie, stop griping. Queenie's a work horse, not a riding horse. You can slide off and walk if you want to."

"No, it's too far to walk. Just don't let her go too fast."

Then some large, biting horse flies spooked her. With her tail flailing, she snorted and started running and jumping to get away from the flies.

"Whoa, back Queenie! Whoa!" Sam yelled in a firm voice, trying to calm her down. "Hang on, Howie."

He pulled back hard on the reins and shouted, "Howie, see if you can smack those horse flies. They really hurt Queenie when they bite."

"Okay, Sam, I got 'em!" Howie shouted after he had smashed two of the large biting flies with his hand. The flies were full of horse blood. He rubbed his bloodied hands on his pants.

After a few more minutes of bouncing up and down Queenie calmed and the ride was smooth. As they approached the woods, Sam slipped off Queenie's back and unlatched the gate. When Queenie with Howie on her back passed through the gate, Sam led her over to a corner of the woods so he could close the gate. As he latched the gate shut he heard a tremendous crash! Queenie let out a frantic whinny. Howie yelled, "Yowie! Yowie! Sam, help me!"

As Sam looked around all he could see through a cloud of dust was the head and neck of Queenie and the face of Howie. He was very pale and frightened. Sam could see that Queenie had fallen into a large hole in the ground and was trying desperately to climb out.

Howie calmed down and, holding on to Queenie's mane, was able to climb out of the hole. Both boys stood like two statutes, silent and dumbfounded, looking at Queenie, not knowing what to do. After a few seconds they came to their senses.

QUEENIE FALLS IN THE WELL

"Howie, run back to the barn and tell dad what happened! I'll stay here with Queenie and try to keep her calm."

Howie took off like an Olympic racer, his shirt tail flying behind. Sam had never seen him run so fast. He got down on his knees in front of Queenie. He held her bridle as he rubbed her nose and stroked her neck. He talked to her trying to get her to relax. Finally, she tired of the struggle and laid her head on the dirt at the edge of the hole.

After a long 30 minutes, Sam looked up to see his dad with Howie and two neighbors racing down the lane toward him in a four-wheeled farm wagon pulled by two large work horses. The lathered and wheezing steeds were galloping at top speed and the wagon was bouncing up and down, making a terrific racket. The horses approached the scene wild-eyed and with nostrils flared and snorting. The wagon and team of horses were barely visible in the swirling dust.

One of the neighbors leaned back on the reins and shouted, "Whoa, Whoa back," as he brought his team and wagon to a stop a short distance from the gate to the woods. Wilmer and the neighbors jumped out of the wagon and ran to where Queenie was struggling to get out of the hole in the ground.

"She's fallen into an old, abandoned dug well!" Wilmer shouted. "Quick, get the shovels out of the wagon. Sam, you keep holding Queenie's bridle. Try to keep her calm."

They got the shovels and began to dig the dirt from the side of the well to form an incline under Queenie's front legs.

"Now, unhitch the horses from the wagon and back 'em up to Queenie," Wilmer shouted at his two neighbors.

They tied ropes around her body back of her front legs and hitched the two ropes to the harness of the neighbor's horses. Wilmer helped Sam hold on to Queenie's bridle.

One of the neighbors took the reins to his team and yelled, "Giddap!" The two large muscular horses lunged forward. Queenie strained and struggled to help herself get up the incline and on level ground. After a few attempts she was up on top again. She was shaking and a little wobbly. Wilmer examined her and said she seemed to be in good shape with no broken bones. The neighbors untied the ropes and hitched the team to the wagon.

Sam looked at Howie and said, "I told you I always come up with some excitement during our exploring adventures!"

"Yeah, but this one ended before it even started," retorted Howie.

"You're right, Howie; we didn't get to do much exploring today. I'm sorry this one turned out to be a dud. But, I've got another adventure in mind that will be really exciting. I'll tell you about it later."

Wilmer tied Queenie's bridle reins to the back of the wagon. Everyone climbed in for the slow, bumpy ride back to the barn. Sam was glad that his dad didn't blame him for Queenie's misfortune.

Wilmer did ask Sam, "What were you going to do back in the woods?"

Sam told him, "We were just exploring. I was going to show Howie some of the animals that hide in the underbrush next to the old rail fences. Remember the mama deer with the baby, and the wild hogs I saw there last summer; and, the opossum, raccoons and....that awful skunk."

Wilmer said, "Hmmmm. Yes, I remember, you smelled like skunk for days. I was glad your bedroom was upstairs."

Then everyone was quiet for several minutes.

Wilmer started to talk with his neighbors. Howie was sitting in the back of the wagon looking at his shoes. Sam sat down next to him. He began to think about Queenie and what had just happened. Then, as usual, his mind began to drift and he began to daydream. Exciting and daring scenes began to drift across his vision as he stared off into space.

CHAPTER 4

SAM'S IMAGINATION

Sam's mind was racing. His imagination kicked in and he was lost in his thoughts. Exciting images began to form in his brain. He saw himself riding his snorting, galloping horse through the countryside, jumping fences and dodging trees. He was firing his BB gun as he chased and finally captured several bad guys with masks covering their faces. He was proud and sat tall in the saddle as he brought the desperados at gun point, tied with rope, into the local jail as the townspeople shouted with approval. The sheriff told Sam how proud he was of him for bringing in several of the worst criminals in the area. Of course, Sam was pleased to claim the large reward mentioned on the wanted poster tacked on the wall in the sheriff's office.

"What are you smiling about, Sam?" asked Howie.

"Oh, nothing," said Sam. He realized that Howie did not have as much imagination.

The wagon slowly bumped along the farm path. Sam's thoughts drifted back a year or two to that time when his family was relaxing in the sitting room one evening after supper. This room was furnished with two large wooden rockers, a library table, a bookcase with glass front, piano, sofa and two smaller rocking chairs.

Millie and Mary were reading stories in the Farm Women's Post and the Women's Country Companion. Wilmer had finished listening to the evening news broadcast over a radio sitting on a table next to his wood rocker. The news program was sponsored by the Green Rocket gasoline and oil company. Rocking slowly, he leafed through the GrantNews, reading the news items, the weather forecast, and the local farm markets.

Every evening after supper Wilmer would settle in his wooden rocker, fill his pipe with Prince Stumble tobacco, tamp it down with his finger, and then scratch a match on his overalls pant leg. He would light the pipe, and Millie would look at him and frown because she thought that tobacco smoke fouled the air in the house. Wilmer blew a cloud of blue smoke toward the light fixture hanging from the ceiling and settled back in his rocker. He let go of the newspaper and, deep in thought, stared at the ceiling. He held his pipe in his lap and soon he was fast asleep.

Sam was sitting nearby in his small red rocker that was a perfect fit for his lanky frame. He grabbed the newspaper as it hit the floor and turned the pages until he came to the comics.

"Let's see what Tru Rider is doing today," he said to himself.

He was a daily reader of the adventures of Tru Rider, a western cowboy who chased and captured dangerous criminals. Tru Rider was a crack shot with his rifle, a lever action, repeating carbine that would zip off shots as fast as he could lever the bullets into the firing chamber. Tru Rider had been Sam's hero for months.

Earlier, Sam had noticed that a store in Manion, the nearest large town to their farm, was selling toy pistols, holsters, and cowboy outfits. He knew that if he could own these cowboy "duds" he would be the Tru Rider of the neighborhood. After considerable pleading, Wilmer and Millie had given him a pistol, holster and cowboy hat as a Christmas present. Wilmer said that Sam was a funny sight wearing his bib overalls, blue shirt, and red bandana across his face, running around trying to terrorize the farm animals with his fake pistol.

As he turned the page of the newspaper, Sam couldn't believe his eyes. There it was, advertised for sale in big bold type; a Tru Rider air rifle…Sam called it a BB gun. It was a lever action carbine, just like Tru Rider's rifle. This was the gun that he just had to own.

"Dad," he shouted, "look at this!"

Wilmer awoke with a start and put his smoldering pipe in the ashtray on the table next to the radio. He leaned over to see what caused Sam's excitement.

"Look at this BB gun. It is just like Tru Rider's, and it cost only a few dollars. This is the gun I want."

Wilmer inhaled, cleared his throat, and looked at the advertisement, then at Sam, and, after several seconds said, "No!" He was always a man of few words.

Sam knew from experience what the word "no" meant. He had wanted a pony when he was eight years old. Every night he had scanned the GrantNews to see if anyone wanted to sell a pony. After months of searching, he finally saw a short notice offering a pony, bridle, saddle and blanket for sale at $40.

"Look here, this pony is just what I have been wanting," he said, as he showed the advertisement to his dad.

Wilmer read it and said, "No!" He explained that they could not afford forty dollars for an animal that did not contribute to farm income. He said that the farm was in a very difficult financial position and they could not afford any extras.

"But, dad," Sam pleaded, "we have room in the barn for the pony. I will work extra hard so that my labor would pay for the $40. Also, we have the old buggy sitting in the catalpa tree grove back of the house just waiting for a steed to pull it around the barnyard."

Sam's imagination was running wild again as he thought about hitching the pony to the buggy and galloping at high speed around the farm. He was standing in front of the driver's seat desperately hanging on to the reins as the buggy rounded the corner of the barn and raced down the farm lane toward the road.

However, Wilmer continued to say "no," and Sam realized that he would never own a pony.

But, even though Wilmer said "no" to the BB gun, Sam kept trying to get him to change his mind over the next several weeks. Sam told him that he could shoot sparrows, rats and pigeons, pests that were known to carry diseases to the livestock.

Also, he told his dad that he was now old enough to learn how to care for and shoot a gun safely. His punch line was that the BB gun did not cost nearly as much as the pony. After two months of pestering,

Wilmer and Millie finally agreed to the purchase. Sam was to pay for the BB gun with money he earned from his 4-H livestock projects.

Wilmer then pointed his finger at Sam and said, "I don't want to see you point any gun at any person or farm animal. If you do, I will take it away from you and lock it up in the gun cabinet."

Wilmer had been in the World War and was very accurate with firearms, including the 22 caliber rifle and the 12 gauge shotgun, now locked in the gun cabinet. He also was very aware of the dangers involved when handling firearms.

"Okay, dad," Sam replied, smiling and happy that he could now be the gun-toting Tru Rider of the neighborhood. Now he could stand a little taller and walk with pride.

Suddenly, one of the wagon wheels hit a deep hole in the path and Sam's thoughts were jolted back to the present. Arriving back at the barn, Howie and Sam led Queenie to the water tank for a drink, and then to her stall in the barn. Sam gave her fresh straw bedding, some hay and a bucket of oats. Wilmer thanked his neighbors for their help in getting Queenie out of the well. Then, they were ready to start the evening chores.

Sam put his arm around Howie's shoulders and told him, "I've got something very important to tell you after supper."

"Okay, but don't tell me you are going to take me back to that woods again. My legs will never be the same after riding on Queenie. No wonder cowboys are so bow-legged."

* * * *

Later that evening after supper, Sam took Howie up to his room. Howie was sitting on the bed and Sam in a chair facing him. He told him about his plan to explore the vacant farm buildings on Grandpa George's property across the road from the HayBend Farm.

"Howie, I've wanted to explore those old buildings for months. They belong to our grandfather George now, but they were built by his mom and dad a long time ago. No one has lived there for ages. The buildings are old, just waiting to be explored. We can take along my BB gun for protection in case we see any strange men lurking in the area."

"Well..., okay," replied Howie, with hesitation, "as long as it isn't too scary. We don't have to ride Queenie do we?"

"No, Howie, we are going to walk."

As they discussed the idea, Sam's imagination was running at full throttle in anticipation of what they might find in the old buildings. Indeed, Sam was more excited about the adventure than Howie.

He went over to the corner of his room, picked up his BB gun and checked it to make sure it wasn't loaded. Then he took a rag and, with affection, wiped off any dust, and polished the wooden stock. Sam handed the gun to Howie.

"Here, Howie, take a look at my B B gun."

After a few minutes, Howie handed it back without comment. He was not interested in guns of any type, or hunting or outdoor sports. Sam was disappointed that Howie's face did not light up with excitement as he examined the BB gun.

"Don't worry, Howie, tomorrow this gun will protect us and we will be able to handle any danger that comes our way."

Howie just grunted.

When he went to bed that night, Sam's mind raced ahead trying to picture what excitement they might find in the old farm buildings across the road. Perhaps they would find a long-hidden treasure of gold coins, left behind years ago by bandits being chased by a sheriff on horseback. As he thought about this he smiled and slowly drifted off to sleep.

CHAPTER 5

EXPLORING THE LOG CABIN

They were up at the crack of dawn. Sam and Howie heard roosters crowing as they dressed hurriedly and ran downstairs, anxious to help Wilmer finish the morning chores. They milked six cows, fed the pigs and gave oats and hay to the horses. Queenie seemed to have recovered from her "trip to the well".

Then, they raced each other back to the house to the appetizing smell of bacon and eggs frying in an iron skillet. Hot steaming biscuits were already on the table waiting for Sam and Howie to add a generous helping of butter and strawberry jam.

As they entered the porch Millie hollered, "You boys take your shoes off out there. They smell like horse manure. Hurry up and wash your hands. Breakfast is ready."

Soon both families were seated and eating. Wilmer asked, "What are you two boys going to do today?"

Sam replied, "We are going to walk down the lane and across the road to explore the buildings on Grandpa George's farm."

Mary was listening to the conversation. She wasn't usually interested in Sam's exploring adventures. In fact, she didn't like to work outdoors. She would rather stay inside and help her mother around the house. Millie had to coax her to go outside and help in planting and tending the vegetable garden. But this time she liked the idea of exploring the long-vacant buildings across the road.

She said loudly, "I want to go along. We studied old log cabins in History class last year. The log cabin across the road on Grandpa's George's farm will give me some ideas for a story next year in school."

"Nah," Sam retorted. "Howie and I want to explore the buildings by ourselves. This isn't a girl thing."

"Mom, tell Sam I can go along."

"Mary, I need you to help me today. We are going to can the tomatoes we picked yesterday. I have sterilized the Mason jars and I am ready to prepare the tomatoes. Perhaps you can join Sam and Howie another day."

"Well...okay," said Mary, a little disappointed, but glad in a way she didn't have to walk through the dusty old buildings.

"Then tomorrow," she continued, "may I ride the bike over to Judy's house and stay for a few days? It's her birthday."

"Yes, that will be fine, Mary," answered her mother. "But be sure you are back here before Uncle Francis and Aunt Lenora leave to go home."

Wilmer had been thinking about Sam and Howie's plan to explore the old buildings across the road. He frowned and put his empty coffee cup on the table. He turned to face both boys and warned, "Son, I want you and Howie to be very careful in those old buildings. They're in bad condition. Don't go up in the hay loft in the barn. The floor up there is old and you could fall right through. Wear shoes and be careful not to step on any rusty nails. Be back here by 12 noon."

Uncle Francis looked up from the morning GrantNews. He leaned over toward Howie and said, "Did you hear what Uncle Wilmer said?"

"Yeah, dad, don't worry, I'll be with Sam."

"We'll be careful," Sam assured Uncle Francis and Wilmer, as he finished off his second biscuit and forked in his last bite of bacon. He wiped his mouth on his red handkerchief and scooted his chair back from the table.

Howie ate more slowly than Sam. While he waited for him to finish, Sam went upstairs to get his BB gun. Wilmer gave him a stern look as he carried the gun through the kitchen. He didn't have to say a word. Sam knew what he was thinking. Then, Sam thought about the flashlight and ran back upstairs to get it. By the time he returned to the kitchen, Howie was about through eating. His third biscuit, smothered with butter and strawberry jam was on its way to his wide open mouth.

"Howie, you've got jam all over your face."

"Okay," said Howie, as he wiped his face with his shirt sleeve.

Lenora looked at Millie and sighed.

"Here, Howie, take the flashlight," Sam said, as he shouldered the BB gun. Then they hurried out to the porch and sat on the floor to put on their shoes. They slammed the door behind them, looking forward to what they might find in the old buildings.

"I'm glad to get those smelly shoes out of the house," said Millie, as she started to clear the dishes from the table.

Sam and Howie walked very fast down the long gravel lane, crossed the road and opened the wooden, slatted gate to the vacant farmstead. Several cows of various size and color were grazing in the grassy fields. The buildings included two large barns, a granary, a log cabin and a more modern home with clapboard siding. All were in bad repair with holes in the roofs, siding boards and windows missing, and doors hanging by one hinge. They entered the barn nearest the road first.

"Maybe we will spot some pigeons or rats," said Sam.

The barn was framed with large hand-hewn timbers, still in good condition after many years of exposure to the weather. The roof and siding, however, were beyond repair. The floor was mostly dirt. The boys noticed some old horse harness hanging on pegs driven into the wall. Howie saw several empty bottles on a weathered shelf. He could still read the labels.

"Dr. Greymares' Horse Liniment, for sore muscles," he said, as he held the bottles up to the light.

In the shed attached to the end of the barn there was an old, broken-down, four-wheeled wagon that had been used to haul grain. The faded green paint was decorated with fancy yellow writing that was still visible. Some of the wheel spokes were missing, making the wagon sag to one side.

"Wow, Howie, can you imagine sitting up there on that wooden seat and driving the four horses that pulled this wagon?"

"How do you know there were four horses?" he asked.

Sam hated to show his superior knowledge about matters like horses, but he had to answer the question. "There are four singletrees lying here on the ground by the wagon tongue. A singletree is this piece of wood and metal that fastens to the tongue of the wagon. It hooks to the horses' harness."

To change the subject, Howie pointed and said, "Come on, Sam, let's go over to the old log cabin."

"Yeah," Sam agreed. "Maybe we can find some excitement there."

"Wait a minute," said Howie. "I think I saw something." He flashed his light into a dark corner of the shed and two beady eyes stared back. "Ýow! What is that?" he exclaimed.

Before Sam could answer, a very large groundhog ran between the boys and disappeared in his burrow under the barn. It happened so quickly that he didn't have time to aim his BB gun.

They then walked quickly through the knee-high grass to the log cabin. They could see it also needed much repair. Some of the roof had fallen in and the door and windows were missing. Trees and shrubs were growing up from the area next to the bottom logs. One large elm tree, growing along the outside of the wall opposite the chimney, seemed to be holding the log cabin upright. Wasp nests seemed to be everywhere. Honey bees and bumblebees were buzzing about their heads, and feeding on the nearby wild flowers.

"How old is this log cabin?" asked Howie, as he smacked a mosquito on his face.

"Dad told me that it was built about 100 years ago by our great grandpa and grandma," replied Sam. "They came from your state of Ohio and built this log cabin here. He said all the building material for the cabin came from this farm. At that time, all of this land was covered with trees."

"Look at this," Sam continued, as they stood next to the chimney on the outside of the cabin. "The chimney was built up from a wide base at ground level, and then it gradually became smaller as it rose above the peak of the roof. It was made of stones, sticks and mud, all from this farm."

"I can't believe this chimney is in such good condition after all of these years," said Howie, rubbing his hands over the surface.

"Let's go inside," Sam said impatiently, as he stepped with caution inside the open door frame with Howie close on his heels.

He held the BB gun ready for any emergency. The only movement, however, was from several birds winging their way out the open windows. They soon realized they were standing in the one and only room in the log cabin. They could see daylight through the cracks between the logs. The floor boards were covered with dust, dirt and bird feathers. Spider webs were everywhere.

"Howie, this is a one-room house."

"Yeah," replied Howie.

They looked around the room, about the size of the sitting room in Sam's home. Smaller logs with boards on top formed the ceiling of the room and the floor of the loft above. Several of these boards had come loose on one end and were hanging down into the main room. Two windows were cut into the logs on one wall. On the opposite wall one window and a door were the only openings. The most obvious feature was located at one end of the room.

Howie shouted, "Wow, look at the size of that fireplace."

He was right. The stone fireplace made up the entire front wall of the room from floor to ceiling. It was built with stones of various sizes right up to the top. There were limestone slabs on the floor in front of the fireplace as a protection against fire from hot embers falling out of the firebox. The inside of the firebox was still covered with black soot from the wood fires of long ago.

"Wow," said Howie again, as they rubbed their hands along the stones. Sam leaned his BB gun up against the log wall as they looked at the fireplace more closely.

"Howie, this room must be where everything happened. This fireplace was used for cooking, heating and gave off some light at night. Just think. If we had been pioneers like our great grandpa and grandma, we could have hunted wild animals in the forest. We could have provided food for the table right here in this room."

"Yeah, I guess so," replied Howie, as he turned to see what else was in the room. Sam could tell that the idea of hunting animals in the forest didn't interest him.

"I can't believe a large family lived here in such a small space," Sam told Howie.

"Why, how many people lived here?"

"My dad said there were eight children and their mom and dad living here until they built the more modern house up on the hill."

"Wow," said Howie. 'Wow' was his favorite expression.

"Look," Sam said, as he pointed to the corner of the room away from the door and opposite the fireplace. "That's what's left of the bed, a few pieces of wood and some rope."

"What was the rope for?"

"The rope was stretched across the wooden bed frame and held up the mattress. The mattress was two pieces of cloth sewed together and stuffed with feathers, corn husks or straw."

"How do you know so much about old beds?"

"Oh, my dad said he slept in a bed like that when he was a small boy," replied Sam.

They left foot prints as they walked on the dusty, well-worn planks that had been the floor of the log cabin to the corner of the room where the bed had been located. Howie pointed to the floor and started to say something about the bed when ...suddenly ...the floor gave way underneath them. With a loud splintering crash both boys tumbled down several feet amid choking dust and fragments of wood.

They both yelled, "Yowie! Yowie! Yowie!"

CHAPTER 6

THE SKELETON

Howie, along with pieces of wood and rope, landed on top of Sam. Luckily, they had fallen only a few feet, but the surprise frightened them so much they were speechless.

"Get off me, Howie," Sam finally demanded. "It's dark down here. Turn on the flashlight."

"I…I...I dropped it," said Howie in a quivering voice.

"Well, feel around until you find it," Sam said, loudly.

After several seconds of silence, Howie yelled, "Here it is."

He turned on the flashlight. As they looked around the dust began to settle. Then…. the sight that met their eyes made their mouths drop open and their eyes bug out.

"W…W…We are in an underground tunnel. Look at those bricks," whispered Sam.

"O…O...Okay," stuttered Howie. "Get out of my way, Sam. I'm getting out of here now!"

"Wait a minute, Howie. Calm down, will you. This is exciting. Let's see where this tunnel goes."

"B…B…But Sam," Howie stammered, "look at all the dust and cobwebs, and see those spider webs. Yikes, there's a humongous spider. And, yikes, look at that big black snake. Sam, he's looking right at me. This place is just too creepy and crawly. I'm getting out of here now!"

As Howie stood to leave, his head reached just above the floor of the log cabin. The tunnel seemed to be about four feet in height and three feet wide. He tried to climb out but couldn't get a foothold so he fell back down in a heap on the damp floor of the tunnel.

"I'm scared, Sam," he moaned, as he picked himself up. "We are trapped down here. We could end up with spider and snake bites. I hate spiders. One bit me on my leg last year when I was helping mom in the garden. My leg swelled up big as a football. Let's get out of here."

"You lived through it didn't you, Howie."

"Yeah, but it hurt like fury."

"Howie, pull yourself together. See, the snake is gone already. This is the reason we came here, to discover, and boy, have we discovered. We've got to see where this tunnel goes."

"But the top of this tunnel might cave in. We could die from suffocation. I'm scared," Howie said with a whimper. "Help me climb out of here, Sam."

"Look," Sam said, trying to be fearless, "the roof of this tunnel hasn't fallen in over the years, has it? So why should it fall in now? Come on. Let's go down a little way in this tunnel to see what we can find. Gee, Howie, this is exciting."

"W…Well, okay," stammered Howie. "But I'm going only a short way. Get rid of that big spider, Sam."

The light from the flashlight shone on Howie's face. Sam could see that his eyes were as big as saucers, his lips were trembling, and his face was very pale. "Let me have the flashlight, Howie," he said softly. "I'll go first."

They could not stand up in the tunnel so they stooped over and bent their legs as they started to creep along the dirt floor. They could see that the sides and top were made of bricks. The top was curved upward toward the center to make the tunnel self-supporting. The dirt floor was damp from water coming in around the bricks. As they moved forward, the dusty cobwebs covered their faces and eyes and got in their mouths.

"Nobody is going to believe us when we tell them about this tunnel," said Sam, as he tried to spit the cobwebs out of his mouth.

After they had gone a few more feet into the tunnel, he added, "I don't believe it myself."

"I still don't trust the top of this tunnel," whispered Howie, as he tried to brush the cobwebs from his face. "And, where did that snake go? Sam, I can't get these dirty cobwebs out of my eyes and mouth. Ugh, how awful. We could be buried alive down here, and no one is here to help us if the top of this tunnel would fall in. Sam, let's go back to your house now," he pleaded.

Sam ignored his cousin. He knew he had to keep Howie's mind busy or he was going to go bonkers. He dropped to his knees and aimed the light forward.

Looking through the cobwebs and dust, they both saw it at the same instant. About ten feet in front of them, highlighted by the flashlight beam, was a jumble of bones, sort of leaning up against one side of the tunnel, as though relaxing after a hard day's work. Remains of a plaid, red and white flannel shirt and blue pants were mixed in with the bones. A faded leather belt with a tarnished metal buckle was lying on the floor of the tunnel close to the skeleton. An old pair of work shoes was lying nearby. A gold ring was still clinging to a finger bone. The metal frame of a pair of glasses had fallen down and became lodged in the rib bones. The remains of a green leather cap still remained tilted on one side of the skull. This pile of bones very much resembled a human skeleton. The skeleton seemed to be saying, 'Hi, boys, I've been waiting for you. What took you so long?' Sam and Howie were fascinated, but also terrified at the sight before their eyes.

Sam was so shaken by the sight he dropped the flashlight.

"Yikes! A skeleton!" yelled Howie. "Yikes! Now I know I'm getting out of here. Yikes, Sam, we've got to go back to your house now."

"W…W…Wait a minute," stuttered Sam, trying to act brave and calm Howie's nerves. "T…T…Those bones….Those bones could be from some large animal, maybe a deer, that wondered down here and couldn't get out. Let's have a closer look."

"D…D…Did you ever see a deer wearing a plaid, red and white flannel shirt; or one running around with a green leather cap on his head?" demanded Howie. "No, Sam, let's get out of here. I want to see daylight."

Picking up the flashlight and shining it on the skeleton, Sam realized that Howie was right. The bones did seem to be human.

As Sam crept closer, Howie sneezed, blowing dust and cobwebs three feet from his face. The sound echoed loudly throughout the tunnel.

"Howie, did you have to do that?" asked Sam, his nerves on edge. "You made me jump and I hit my head on the top of the tunnel."

They edged closer, their eyes fixed on the skull. They could see that the skull was not from an animal....it seemed to be.....it looked like it was human. Then they both suddenly realized this heap of bones at one time could have been a living, breathing, talking person.

Now Sam was as frightened as Howie. "Let's get out of here. I'm going to tell my dad what we've found. He'll know what to do. Howie, back up so we can get out of here."

Just as they were ready to back out of the tunnel the flashlight beam fell on a metal object lodged in the bones of one hand of the skeleton. "Look at that, Howie. What is that piece of metal held by the finger bones of the skeleton?"

"I don't know and I don't care!" yelled Howie, as he started to crawl backwards. "I'm getting out of this dark and creepy tunnel now, this very minute."

"Okay, but I'm taking that piece of metal the skeleton is holding with me to show my dad."

CHAPTER 7

THE GIANT HORSESHOE

The tunnel was completely dark except for the pencil-like beam of the flashlight pointing toward the bony left hand of the skeleton. Sam's hand was shaking wildly as he slowly reached out and gently lifted the object from the finger bones. In his mind he was afraid the skeleton would rise up and yell, 'Don't take that. It's mine!'

"Howie, take the flashlight. I've got the piece of metal."

They quickly backed out of the tunnel to the opening in the log cabin floor. Sam reached up and placed the piece of metal on the cabin floor.

"Here, Howie put your foot in my hands and I can boost you up."

When he was up on the cabin floor Howie grabbed Sam's hand and pulled him up. They could hardly stand up. They were still trembling and unsteady on their feet. They were now up in the log cabin and the sunlight let them see their surroundings. They looked around the room, then at each other. Pointing, they burst out laughing. Their shirts, pants, hands and faces were covered with dirt and cobwebs. Their eyes were like white marbles, floating in a sea of grime. Their shoes were wet and covered with mud. Their hair was caked with dust and cobwebs. They looked like visitors from another world.

However, both Sam and Howie were now feeling more at ease since they were up and out of the dark tunnel. Their nerves gradually calmed and their voices returned to normal. They became steadier on their feet. Sam stooped over and picked up the metal object that had been held by the left hand of the skeleton. He looked at it more closely.

"Howie, this is a horseshoe."

"No way, it's too big. No horse has feet that big."

Then Sam realized Howie was right. But the piece of metal was in the shape of a horseshoe.

"Howie," Sam shouted, "we have found a giant horseshoe!"

"Okay, so we found a big horseshoe. Now let's get out of here," responded Howie, as he started walking toward the door of the log cabin. It was obvious that Howie didn't think the horseshoe was a very important discovery.

Sam looked at his pocket watch. It was almost 12 noon. "Okay, I'm ready."

With horseshoe in one hand, Sam picked up his BB gun with his other hand. They rushed out of the log cabin door, ran back to the gate, raced across the road and down the farm lane to Sam's house. Sam tossed the giant horseshoe on the porch floor. They burst into the kitchen, exhausted, gasping for breath, and sprawled out on two chairs by the dining table. Millie's eyes widened and her jaw dropped. She stopped abruptly in the middle of ironing one of Wilmer's shirts. She frowned, faced the boys and put her fists on her hips.

"Where have you boys been? Look at you. You are both filthy. Get out of this kitchen and back to the porch now. Take off those muddy shoes. And, get those dirty clothes off!" she yelled, her voice booming throughout the house.

Aunt Lenora was frying chicken in a large iron skillet on the kerosene stove. She mopped her sweating brow with her apron and looked up to see why Millie was so mad and excited. When she spotted Howie, she could not recognize him, his face was so dirty. "Howie, you look simply awful. How could you get so dirty in just four hours? Now, quickly, do as Aunt Millie says."

Millie, Lenora and Mary had finished canning the tomatoes. Twelve quart containers of whole tomatoes and six quarts of tomato juice sat on the kitchen table waiting to be stored in the cool basement.

Mary took one look at Sam and Howie and said, "I'm sure glad

I didn't go with you this morning. You both are a real mess. And you both really stink. Did you step in some cow poop?"

The tone and volume of Millie's voice completely dampened the boy's enthusiasm. They forgot the reason for their haste and, with shoulders slumped, slowly shuffled off to the porch to take off their shoes and clothes. Howie tried to get his pants off over his shoes.

"Howie, why don't you take off your shoes first?"

He looked at Sam, nodded, and sat down on the floor to remove his shoes. The excitement of the morning had made both boys rather befuddled.

As Sam stood there in his underwear, he glanced at the giant horseshoe that he had dropped on the porch floor. Then, he remembered. "Mom," he shouted. "Look at what Howie and I found at the old log cabin across the road.....a giant horseshoe."

Millie sighed. She had heard this type of excitement before when Sam returned from his exploring adventures. Once last year, he had brought home a large, curved tooth. He said it was from some prehistoric animal. Wilmer said it was a tooth from a male hog.

She placed the iron on its end and walked out to the porch, took one look at the piece of metal and turned on her heel to return to her ironing board.

"Many people have found old horseshoes on farms for years," she said. "There's nothing special about that one. Put your dirty clothes in that basket. And, throw your shoes outside. They need a good scrubbing." She continued ironing. She looked at Lenora, raised her eyebrows and shrugged her shoulders.

Sam and Howie looked at each other, deflated, dirty and disappointed.

"Now, both of you boys get to the bathroom and get cleaned up. Use soap and wash your faces and ears. Get that dirt out of your hair. Put on clean clothes....and don't leave the bathroom in a mess. Dinner will be ready in a few minutes."

They marched like two defeated warriors into the bathroom.

Wilmer had installed modern fixtures a few years ago, including a toilet, bathtub and sink with hot and cold running water. Millie had so thoroughly scolded them that Sam and Howie had completely forgotten about their discovery of the tunnel and the skeleton. When they soaped up and scrubbed the dirt from their faces, however, they both remembered.

"Howie, hurry up. We've got a lot of talking to do," Sam said, as he pulled on a clean blue shirt and a fresh pair of bib overalls. "And, you didn't get your ears clean."

"Okay," said Howie, as he gave his head another scouring. "I'll be right there."

At the noon dinner table Sam and Howie could hardly wait to tell their thrilling story of discovery. Sam started to talk several times but Uncle Francis was rattling on about a new variety of seed corn. He said the new variety would increase Wilmer's corn yield ten bushels per acre. Sam didn't know it took so long to explain a certain kind of corn. He kept fidgeting in his chair, waiting for Francis to end his chatter.

The meal was nearly over and Sam was afraid he wasn't going to be able to tell his story. Finally, Uncle Francis stopped talking long enough to take a big bite of fried chicken, and Sam jumped in.

"Dad," he said, almost yelling, "you won't guess what Howie and I found this morning at the old log cabin across the road."

"You don't need to shout, son, we are sitting right here beside you," Wilmer replied. "No, I can't imagine what you two got into today, especially after letting Queenie fall into that old dug well yesterday. Do tell us," he said with a grin, wiping his mouth with his red handkerchief. He looked at Millie. She was also smiling.

Mary was looking with interest at Sam. She had to admit he could hold her attention when he told a story.

"Well, it's like this," Sam started. He sounded self-assured.

Sam hesitated. Wilmer smiled again and said, "Go on, son." He knew from past experience that Sam could make a story very interesting, with wild gestures and vivid facial expressions. Also, if Sam talked he didn't have to listen to Uncle Francis chatter on about seed corn. "What dragons have you killed this time? Have you discovered another tooth from a prehistoric dinosaur?"

The words started to just gush out of Sam's mouth.

"We took the BB gun and a flashlight this morning to the old buildings across the road. We thought we might see some rats or pigeons. First, we explored the big barn by the road. We found some old harness hanging on one wall. We found an old farm wagon in a shed attached to the end of the barn. Then, we walked over to the log cabin."

Sam was sitting on the edge of his chair. He waited a few seconds and looked around to make sure he had the attention of everyone, including Uncle Francis, and then he continued. "We looked at the big chimney on the outside wall of the log cabin. Then we went inside and examined the large stone fireplace for a long time. Did you know that the log cabin has only one room?"

"Yes, I know that, Sam," said Wilmer. "Did you boys see the narrow, wooden, spiral stairway leading to the sleeping loft above? That's where all the older children slept."

"No, because of what I'm going to tell you next, dad," Sam replied excitedly, squirming in his chair.

"Well, go on. Don't keep us in suspense."

Uncle Francis cleared his throat loudly, indicating he wanted to say something. Sam knew he had to keep talking if he was ever going to finish his story before Uncle Francis interrupted. He was so excited he was now half standing and half sitting on his chair, with fork in one hand and spoon in the other hand.

Finally, leaning forward and pointing with his fork, he continued in a loud voice. "Howie and I were standing in the corner of the log cabin where the bed had been located when all of a sudden, the floor gave way and we fell …down…..into a tunnel!"

Wilmer dropped his fork and it clattered on the kitchen floor, coming to rest under the cooking stove. Everyone, including Uncle Francis, stopped chewing, became quiet and looked in Sam's direction with questioning eyes.

The clock on the wall ticked loudly.

Howie shuffled his feet under the table.

Uncle Francis cleared his throat again.

Mary looked at Sam with disbelief and disgust. She was sure he was just showing off. Sometimes she could just bop him on top of the head.

Millie nervously wiped her mouth with her apron.

"What!" shouted Wilmer, "A tunnel under that log cabin? That is preposterous!"

Sam didn't know what that big word meant, but he knew from his tone of voice his dad didn't believe him.

Then Wilmer started talking, still with a loud voice, "I am forty years old and have lived in this area all my life. I have never heard of such a thing as a tunnel under any building. And, something else, my father has lived here all his life and he has never said anything about a tunnel. No, son, I'm sure you boys fell into a hole in the ground where rain has washed away the soil over the years. No, son, I would have known if there is a tunnel under that log cabin."

"Dad, I'm telling you the truth. I know the difference between a hole in the ground and a tunnel. Tell 'em, Howie."

Howie straightened up in his chair. "Yep," he said, with uncommon confidence, "we both fell through the cabin floor with a loud crash and landed in a tunnel lined with bricks. It was creepy and scary, with dirt, dust, spiders, snakes and cobwebs. It was pitch black. I was scared to death and wanted to come home right away but Sam made me stay. It's a tunnel all right."

Everyone was quiet, looking at Sam and Howie.

The clock seemed to tick louder.

Now that Sam had the attention of everyone around the table, he decided to drop the next bombshell. He was enjoying the moment.

"Guess what we found in the tunnel?"

Sam knew everyone was looking at him and he wanted to make the most of it. He waited a few more seconds to increase the suspense. The kitchen was deathly quiet. The only sound was heavy breathing and the loud 'tick-tock, tick-tock' of the clock on the wall.

Mary was disgusted. She knew Sam just wanted attention. She tried to kick him under the table to get him to shut up but her legs weren't long enough to reach him.

"Well?" asked Millie loudly.

Then he blurted it out, "We found a skeleton!"

This time Uncle Francis's jaw dropped and he lost his fork. It bounced on the floor ending up under the sink. "Well, I'll be plague gone." That was his favorite saying.

Then Sam's mom came up for air. "Sam, you found a what, a skeleton? It must be a skeleton of a cat or a dog, or maybe a deer. You don't mean a skeleton of a person, do you?"

"I don't know, mom, but the skull sure looks human to me. And, there are some remains of a man's clothing mixed in with the bones. Tell her, Howie."

"Yep, Aunt Millie, the bones are leaning up against the wall of the tunnel, sort of lazy like. What's left of a red and white shirt and blue pants is mixed in with the bones. And the skull is wearing a faded green leather cap."

"Oh," she declared, as she pictured the skeleton in her mind. She twisted her apron with her hands. "What can we do? Oh me. Wilmer, do something. Do something."

"Calm down, dear," Wilmer replied, as he scooted backwards and heaved himself out of his chair. "I will go with the boys this afternoon to the log cabin. We will solve this mystery of the so-called tunnel once and for all." He looked at Millie with a sparkle in his eyes and said, "And, I am anxious to see that skeleton wearing a red and white shirt, blue pants and a green leather cap."

Millie thought she detected a slight smirk on Wilmer's face.

He grabbed his hat from a hook on the porch wall and started toward the door. He was sure that Sam's ever present imagination had overcome reason and reality. He muttered to himself, "I'll show these boys there is no tunnel and no human skeleton under that log cabin."

CHAPTER 8

THE CLUES

Sam and Howie were excited. They were anxious to show Wilmer they were serious explorers who had made an important discovery. They picked up their shoes from the lawn outside, wiped them clean on the grass and brought them inside the porch. As Sam sat on the floor lacing up his shoes, he looked over and saw the large metal horseshoe.

"Dad," he said, as he stood up and pulled on Wilmer's shirt sleeve.

"What?" his dad asked, rather impatiently.

"I want to show you something else. See this horseshoe. We found it in the bony, left hand of the skeleton."

Wilmer stopped and reached for the horseshoe. "Let's see that!" he demanded. He turned the horseshoe over and over in his hands. After a few seconds, he said, "They don't raise horses that big around here. That's just a piece of metal that's shaped like a horseshoe. I would say it's a piece of useless junk." He tossed it on the floor and walked out the door.

The impact jarred some of the rust loose from the horseshoe. Sam thought he could see some markings on the flat side. He bent over for a closer look. "No, I guess not," he muttered to himself. "It's probably nothing."

"Come on, boys. I've got a lot of work to do in the barn this afternoon, so I have to get back soon. Let's go have a look at this so-called tunnel and lazy skeleton. Bring along your flashlight."

Wilmer was in a hurry, and his longer legs made Sam and Howie run to keep up. He kept talking softly to himself all the way down the long lane. "It can't be. My father would have told me about any tunnel under that cabin. There's no possible reason for a tunnel to be located under that log cabin. No, it's just a hole in the ground, that's what it is. And, I'll prove it to Sam and Howie. And that pile of bones can't be a human skeleton," he mumbled, as he tried to convince himself.

They passed through the gate and walked rapidly through the high grass to the cabin. The cows grazing nearby looked up with curiosity, then continuing munching away.

"Watch out where you're stepping, Howie," said Sam, as he remembered his mother's tongue lashing.

Wilmer barged in through the door of the cabin and walked immediately to the corner of the room where the hole in the floor was located. Howie and Sam were right behind.

"Let me have the flashlight," he said. He leaned over the opening and directed the light down and around the hole. Then he saw the bricks lining the opening to the tunnel.

"Jumpin' Lizards!" he exclaimed. "You were right about those bricks. You boys may be on to something. I'm going down for a closer look." He jumped down into the hole, dropped to his knees and aimed the light in the direction of the tunnel.

"Jumpin' Lizards!" he said again. "Well, I'll be…It sure does look like a tunnel alright…I can't believe it… I just can't believe it. I'm going to crawl down this tunnel a little ways. You boys wait for me up there."

Sam and Howie got down on their hands and knees at the edge of the hole in the floor. They stuck their heads down to see if Wilmer was able to crawl into the tunnel.

It was quiet except for Wilmer's heavy breathing and his knees scraping along the bottom of the tunnel. Then, after several minutes, the boys heard Wilmer yell, "Jumpin' Lizards! Jumpin' Lizards!" The words rebounded back and forth through the tunnel and came up through the opening in the cabin floor to their ears.

"Howie," Sam said, "he's found the skeleton."

Wilmer scooted rapidly backwards to the hole in the floor. He raised his head up to where Sam and Howie were seated cross-legged on the floor. His face was pale and his brow arched upward. His voice trembled.

His hand shook as he handed the flashlight to Sam and said, "Son, you and Howie are absolutely right. That does seem to be a human skeleton in there. We have a very serious situation here on your Grandpa George's property. I'm going to town now and talk to Sheriff Neverfine." Sam and Howie reached down and helped him up to the cabin floor.

Wilmer and the boys rushed out of the cabin door and walked quickly to the gate, scattering the cows in all directions. They practically ran down the lane to the house. Wilmer, out of breath, jumped in the family Chevrolet, turned the key, and stomped on the starter button. The engine roared to life.

"I wish they would hurry up and string those phone lines out here so we could just call the sheriff, instead of driving seven miles to town," uttered Wilmer.

"Tell mom where I'm going," he yelled out the open car window, as he sped down the lane, sending loose gravel flying out from the rear of the car. Wilmer was usually a very slow, cautious driver. This time he was going to make the trip to Manion in record time.

While they waited for Wilmer to return, Howie and Sam picked up the giant horseshoe from the porch floor and took it to the farm shop to examine it more closely. It was indeed too large to fit the hoof of a horse, and the ends were bent down at a right angle. Sam took a hammer and tapped the metal to loosen more rust.

"Look at this, Howie. There ARE marks on the flat side! Let's get a brush and some water and try to get more of this rust off." After a lot of rubbing and tapping, the marks became more visible.

"See, here at the top of the horseshoe, Howie. This mark looks like a box with a roof. It looks like a tiny house. And, below the house on the right side of the horseshoe is the outline of…it looks like…. a fireplace. It looks just like the fireplace in the log cabin."

"Look, there's a mark between the house and the fireplace that looks like a star…. with four points!" said Howie with excitement, as he pointed to the side of the metal. "And, right below the star is an arrow pointing down."

"Yeah… we'll have to show this to dad when he gets back," Sam said as he placed the horseshoe on the workbench. "Let's go to the house and get some root beer to drink. I'm thirsty."

"Yeah, me too," said Howie.

"Take off your shoes outside, Howie," suggested Sam, as they walked toward the house.

While they were slurping their root beer at the kitchen table, Sam's mom began to fire one question after another at them. She had been discussing the discovery of the tunnel and the skeleton with Lenora.

"What did you find? Where did dad go? When would he be back? Is there really a tunnel? What about the skeleton? Is it a human skeleton?" Millie asked, as she twisted her apron in her hands.

"Yes, mom, there is a tunnel. Yes, there is a skeleton. It does look like a human skeleton. Dad went to town to talk to Sheriff Neverfine, and he should be back soon," Sam explained.

Millie, still very nervous and tense, returned to snapping the green beans she was preparing for supper that evening

Just as they were draining the second glass of root beer, Wilmer returned. He drove up the driveway at a slow speed and parked near the rear porch door. He slammed the car door and walked slowly into the house with his hands in his pockets.

"Well?" asked Millie.

Wilmer poured himself a full glass of cold root beer and took a long drink. He looked at her, sat down on a chair and threw his hands up in the air. "I did go to see Sheriff Neverfine. He was busy asking two strangers a lot of questions. I overheard some of the conversation.

It seems that he has had complaints that two men were on our neighbor's property without permission. As the sheriff was driving out to investigate, he spotted two men in a black car. He stopped the car and brought the two men in to the jail for questioning because they matched the descriptions given by our neighbor. I noticed one of the men had long red hair and the other man had dark hair.

The sheriff saw I was waiting outside the door to his office. He came out and I told him about the tunnel and the skeleton. He was very surprised but seemed to be interested in the information I gave him. He said he would be out in the morning to see for himself."

Sam spoke up. "Dad, you said one of the men had red hair. Do you think they could be the same men who almost ran over Mary as she crossed the road to get the mail?"

"Hmmmm, I hadn't thought about that," said Wilmer. "It's possible, I suppose. We'll keep it in mind."

Sam tugged at his father's shirt sleeve. "Dad, Howie and I have something to show you. It's out in the shop. That giant horseshoe has some strange marks on the flat side."

Wilmer looked at Millie and shrugged his shoulders. He placed his empty root beer glass on the kitchen table. As he walked to the farm shop with Sam and Howie, he said, "Boys, the exploring you did this morning across the road sure is turning into a worrisome but exciting mystery. I'm anxious to hear what the sheriff says when he comes out in the morning to look at that tunnel."

The giant horseshoe was lying on top of the shop workbench. Sam picked it up and handed it to his dad. "See," he said, "this mark looks like a small house and this one looks like a fireplace."

"And, there is a star with four points in between those two marks," added Howie.

"Hmmmm...yes, I see." Wilmer replied, as he brought the metal up closer to his eyes. "And, here an arrow points from the house to the fireplace, if you hold the horseshoe with the curved part on top, and the open part on the bottom. The ends are turned under at a right angle. All the marks seem to be on the right hand side of the horseshoe. That's strange. Let's see if we can rub off more of the rust. Hand me that wire brush, Sam."

Wilmer began to strongly rub the metal with the wire brush. "Look at this," he said, with some excitement. "See these other figures stamped in the metal. This one is a rectangle. It looks like a box with a lid."

Sam and Howie's eyes were wide as the three of them leaned over the workbench to see if there were any more marks on the giant horseshoe.

Sam pointed and said, "Look, there's something below the fireplace figure."

"It's another star!" yelled Howie loudly. "This one has five points." Sam had to give Howie credit for that discovery. Neither he nor his dad had noticed the second star

"And, right below that star is a line with a point on the end. It looks like an arrow pointing to the right," added Howie.

"Yeah," said Sam. "Then we have the rectangle that looks like a box."

Suddenly, Howie blurted out, "There's something else just below the rectangle. It looks like a star too, with more than five points. Count 'em, Sam. There are eight points."

"You're right, Howie," said Wilmer slowly. "Let's see what we have here. First, there's the figure that looks like the little house, then a star with four points and arrow pointing toward the fireplace. Second, there's a figure that looks like a fireplace. Below the fireplace is a star with five points, with arrow pointing to the right. Next is the rectangle that looks like a box with lid. And finally, we have a star with eight points."

Wilmer said softly, as if to himself, "Why would anyone go to the trouble to make all these deep marks on a piece of metal in the shape of a horseshoe? Well, that seems to be it," he said, as he put away the wire brush. "I don't see any more marks on either side of the horseshoe. Let's get some paper and a pencil and make a diagram of what we have discovered."

Sam ran to the house. He soon returned with a large sheet of paper and a stubby pencil from his school supply. They placed the horseshoe on the paper and traced a line to outline the metal. Then they drew in the figures that were marked on the metal surface.

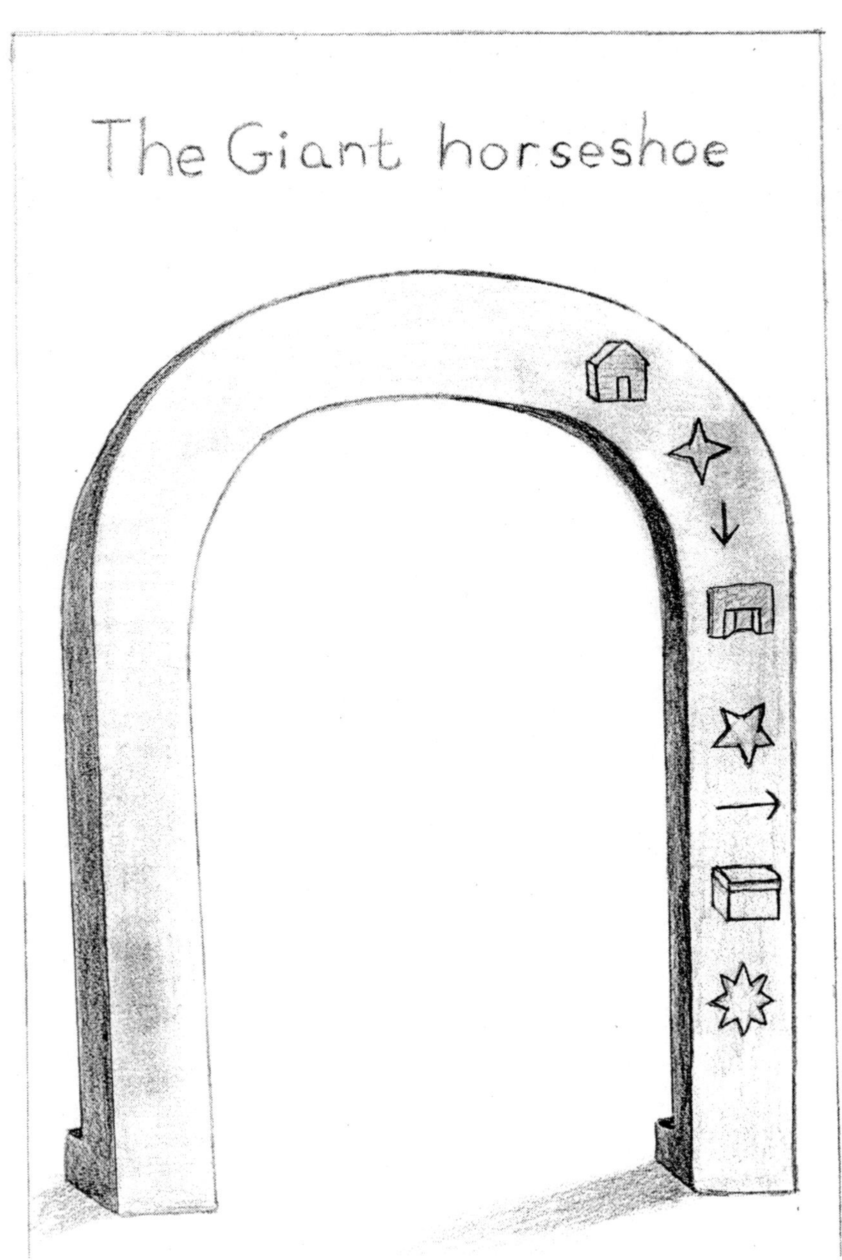

THE GIANT HORSESHOE

"And to think, this piece of metal was held by one hand of the skeleton. This is a real mystery," said Wilmer, his voice trailing off. "Well, it's getting late. I have some work to do in the barn and then I'll feed the animals. Let's think about these marks on this giant horseshoe and sleep on it. Maybe we'll have some ideas tomorrow as to what these marks mean. It could be a prank. The marks probably don't mean a thing. Even if they do, this happened a long time ago and they probably have no meaning for us today."

Although Sam and Howie had to agree the marks on the metal were a mystery, they were still excited about their discovery. After supper that evening in Sam's bedroom they turned the giant horseshoe over and over trying to make sense of the marks. They talked a long time between themselves as to the possible meanings of the markings. Finally, Howie said, "Sam, I'm sleepy. Let's talk about it tomorrow."

"Okay, but I think the marks on this giant horseshoe are clues that will help us solve this mystery. But, what are they telling us?"

Slowly, Sam drifted off to sleep with the giant horseshoe resting in his hands.

CHAPTER 9

SHERIFF NEVERFINE INVESTIGATES

The next morning, Sam and Howie were awakened by loud talking. The voices were coming from outside their bedroom window. Looking out, they saw the sheriff's car parked in the driveway.

"Howie, look at that car," Sam said loudly, as he pointed out the window. "It's a shiny, black one! It looks like a Ford. Look, there's a spotlight by the driver's window, and look at those whitewall tires. And, there's a siren on the front fender."

"Yeah," responded Howie, as he leaned his head and shoulders outside the window for a better look. "Wow! She's a beaut all right. Look at that yellow star painted on the driver's door. I'll bet she'll do a hundred."

Sheriff Neverfine had been involved in law enforcement for many years. He had been a deputy sheriff for ten years before being elected sheriff of Grantor County three years ago. Before that he was a policeman for the city of Manion. A large man weighing at least 250 pounds and over six feet in height, he was now gaining weight around his middle. At 50 years of age his curly blond hair was beginning to reflect specks of grey. His rosy, chubby cheeks helped to hold up a small pair of round, wire-rimmed eye glasses.

His tan uniform was always neatly pressed, with sharp creases on the shirt sleeves and trouser legs. A dark brown tie and sheriff's star highlighted a shirt that struggled to contain his barrel-shaped chest. His black shoes always carried a mirror-like shine. When he placed his meaty right hand on his holster containing his service revolver, he was indeed a figure that made other people feel less important, especially the prisoners in his jail cells.

As the boys gawked at the car and the sheriff, they could hear part of the conversation. Sheriff Neverfine was talking to Wilmer and Millie about the tunnel and the skeleton.

"Come on, Howie," yelled Sam, "let's get down there."

They jumped into their clothes and bounded down the stairs three steps at a time. As they rushed through the kitchen they put a handful of oatmeal cookies in their pockets, then grabbed their shoes from the porch floor and ran out the door to where Wilmer, Millie and the sheriff were standing. They sat on the grass to put on their shoes.

"So, you are the two boys who found the tunnel and the skeleton under the log cabin," Sheriff Neverfine stated, with disbelief in his voice. He found it hard to believe two young boys without police training could make such an important discovery.

"We haven't had any missing persons in this area of the state for several years. You boys probably found the skeleton of an animal. I doubt very much if it's human, but to satisfy your curiosity we'll go to the log cabin and look around anyway." Sam could tell from the sheriff's tone of voice that he thought his trip to the farm was a waste of his time and talents.

Sam and Howie finally got their shoes on and tied. They joined Wilmer as they all piled into the sheriff's car. Wilmer sat up front. Sam and Howie sat on the edge of the back seat, their eyes fixed on the sawed-off shotgun strapped across the top of the dashboard. They looked at each other with excitement. This was the first time either of them had been in a police car. Howie saw the police radio and poked Sam in the ribs as he pointed toward the dashboard.

Sam whispered, "Yeah."

Sheriff Neverfine squeezed his large stomach in behind the steering wheel, slammed the door and stepped on the starter button. The black Ford, with the powerful V-8 engine, roared to life as if eager to race toward the road in front of the farm.

"You boys might want to clean up those shoes when we get back. You're making this car smell like a cow pen," said the sheriff, with a bit of authority in his voice.

As the sheriff drove down the lane Sam leaned over to Howie and whispered, "He'll have trouble fitting into the tunnel. He's too big."

Howie nodded.

Parking beside the road in front of Grandpa George's vacant farmstead, they got out of the car and walked slowly toward the log cabin. The sheriff was not a fast walker.

"Did you find out any information about the two strangers who were in your office yesterday?" Wilmer asked, as he walked beside the sheriff.

"Not much. I had to let them go. I had to realize there is more than one man in this county with red hair. There was not enough evidence to connect them to the burglary down the road from here at the Katchnot place. As for the trespassing charge, they denied ever being on the property. I told them it would be best if they returned to Kentucky where they said they came from."

The sheriff, his eyes fixed on the log cabin, stepped in a big pile of cow poop. "Well, boys," he said, rather quietly, "it looks like I'll have to clean my shoes too." Sam and Howie looked at each other and tried to quiet their laughter with their hands.

By this time they were at the log cabin door. "This place is a mess," muttered the sheriff, as he cautiously stepped through the open door frame into the cabin. "Okay, where's the tunnel?" he asked, impatiently.

"Over here," said Sam, as he ran ahead and pointed to the hole in the log cabin floor.

Sheriff Neverfine took off his hat, gun belt and holster and placed them on the floor. With flashlight in hand, he dropped down into the hole with a thud. "Well, I'll declare! It sure looks like a tunnel alright," he said loudly, with surprise in his voice. "I didn't expect to see these bricks. You boys may be right. I'm going to crawl down here a ways. Wait for me up there… And, you boys keep your hands off that holster and gun."

He got down on his hands and knees and slowly began to work his way into the tunnel. They could hear his grunts as he moved forward.

Sam and Howie were crouched down at the edge of the opening in the floor trying to see if the sheriff was making any progress. After a few minutes, they heard a loud yell that bounced back to the opening in the floor of the cabin.

"Howie," Sam said, "he's found the skeleton!"

It took a long time for Sheriff Neverfine to scoot back out of the tunnel. They knew he was getting close to the hole in the log cabin floor because his grunts, groans and heavy breathing were getting louder. Finally, his rear end appeared. Wilmer, Sam and Howie all reached down and helped pull him up to the cabin floor.

"That's a real human skeleton in there or an excellent fake!" said the sheriff loudly, as he brushed the dirt and cobwebs off his neatly pressed tan uniform. "To say I'm surprised is putting it mildly. You two boys have stumbled on to something here. Let's go," he said, as he picked up his hat and gun belt and headed for the door. Everyone was quiet as they quickly walked back and climbed into the sheriff's car.

They sat there silently in the car for several minutes. The only sound was the sheriff's heavy breathing. Finally, he spoke, "Sam and Howie, you have made an important and upsetting discovery! This mystery is too much for me. I'm going to call in some experts from the Indiana State Police. They can take pictures and remove the skeleton for analysis."

Sam looked at Howie and asked, "What does analysis mean?"

He just shrugged his shoulders.

The sheriff overheard the question. He answered, "Analysis is an attempt by the state police to find out everything possible about the skeleton. They will try to determine if it's male or female, how long it has been in the tunnel and the cause of death. They will also try to put a name on the skeleton."

The sheriff talked softly to himself as he drove back to Wilmer's house. "Maybe it was stolen from a high school biology laboratory or a medical college. That doesn't seem likely because of the pieces of clothing mixed in with the bones. But, how did the skeleton get into the tunnel? Could this be a teen-age prank? Or worse yet, was someone injured or killed outside and then left in the tunnel many years ago? Or, was someone hiding in the tunnel and then died? Was this death due to natural causes or… was it murder? Under the circumstances it is going to be very difficult to determine the identity of the skeleton. This is really a mystery."

Sam and Howie looked at each other with raised eyebrows.

The sheriff was so deep in thought he almost ran over some chickens wandering in the barnyard. As Wilmer and the boys got out of the car he said, "You will hear from me, probably tomorrow." He was still mumbling to himself as he sped down the lane on his return trip to town.

They continued to stand there, stunned by the sheriff's comments. Sam was the first to speak. "Did you hear him say murder?"

"Yes, I did," replied Wilmer. "This situation is becoming very alarming. I'm glad the sheriff and the state police are taking the responsibility for removing the skeleton. Now you boys can think about the meaning of those marks on the giant horseshoe. Also, we need to find out why there is a tunnel under that log cabin. In the meantime, we have work to do. After dinner you boys can help me move the pigs from the front pasture to the lot back of the barn. The veterinarian will be here soon to vaccinate them for cholera."

* * * *

The next day Sheriff Neverfine returned to HayBend Farm and reported that the Indiana State Police and their laboratory people would remove and take possession of the skeleton the following morning. He asked that no one enter the tunnel until after the skeleton is removed.

By this time the editor of the GrantNews had heard about the discovery of the tunnel and skeleton. He sent a reporter to the HayBend Farm to get information from Sam's parents. The reporter parked his car in the shade of one of the maple trees in front of the house. Wilmer and Millie came out of the house and answered his many questions. The boys joined them and listened in but kept quiet.

Finally, Sam's dad said, "You need to talk to these two boys, Sam and Howie. They discovered the tunnel and the skeleton."

The reporter got another note pad and pencil from his car. He suggested they sit down on the grass in the shade of one of the maple trees. Sam and Howie spent the next hour explaining their discovery and how they found the skeleton. Toward the end of the conversation Howie thought about the giant horseshoe and started to blurt out, "and the skeleton was holding…" Sam kicked him in the shins and motioned for him to keep quiet.

The boys then took the reporter to the log cabin where he took some photographs of them in front of the cabin, and of the tunnel entrance. Sam told him no one was to enter the tunnel until after the skeleton was removed.

"I have to get back now to the press room and write up this story for tomorrow's newspaper. It's going to be a very good interest article," he said, as he thanked the boys and dropped them off at the house. His car was soon lost in the dust as he sped away.

"Why did you kick me, Sam, when I started to tell him about the giant horseshoe?"

"Because, Howie, that's our secret. Besides, we don't know what the marks on the horseshoe mean, or where the tunnel ends. Tomorrow morning the state police are removing the skeleton and then we can look at the rest of the tunnel. Every tunnel leads somewhere. I want to see where this one ends!"

"Oh….Okay, I'll be ready," said Howie with a sigh.

That night, up in Sam's room, he and Howie were in deep thought about the giant horseshoe. "Howie, why would anyone make a horseshoe that is too big for a horse? And, why go to the trouble to hammer those marks on the flat side? I think those marks are trying to tell us something about this mystery."

"Nah," responded Howie, "your imagination is running wild again. Some blacksmith had some extra time and decided to make a special horseshoe to advertise his shop."

"Well, maybe so," Sam replied, "but how did it end up in the bony hand of a skeleton in that tunnel on Grandpa George's property? I'm going to take it with us tomorrow afternoon when we go back to explore the tunnel. Maybe we can figure out if the marks on the giant horseshoe are clues that will help us solve this mystery."

"Oh, okay, Sam, but right now I'm tired. I'm going to sleep."

Soon Howie was fast asleep. Sam, however, was wide awake for an hour trying to imagine how the skeleton, the giant horseshoe and the tunnel under the log cabin all could fit together as a solution to the mystery.

* * * *

The next day dawned hot and without a breeze. Fluffy clouds decorated the deep blue sky. The morning chores were completed. Oatmeal, toast, apple jelly and milk were on the table ready for breakfast. Sidney had delivered the GrantNews. The adults were enjoying a final cup of strong coffee. Sam had picked up the newspaper from the mailbox. Everyone gathered around the kitchen table as Wilmer spread the paper out for all to see.

"There we are, Howie," Sam exclaimed. "We're right on the front page. Look at that."

The headline read:

HUMAN SKELETON FOUND IN
TUNNEL ON FARM EAST OF CITY!!

A two-column story, below several pictures, was featured at the top of the page under the headline. Sam was pictured in his bib overalls and Howie with his shirt tail hanging out. They were standing in front of the log cabin with big grins on their faces. The reporter had written the story as a mystery ending with a lot of the same questions the sheriff had mentioned.

"Wow," said Howie, "we're famous!"

"We'll be even more famous if we make any more discoveries in that log cabin," Sam replied.

"Or, in the tunnel," added Howie.

Wilmer heard the boys talking. He turned to face both Sam and Howie. "Listen here," he said in a stern voice, "you boys need to be careful this afternoon. I know the tunnel looks safe, but it's old and some of the bricks may be broken or washed away.

Also, the state police are removing the skeleton this morning. They may damage the walls and make them weaker. I want only one of you in the tunnel at one time. That way, if there is trouble the other person can come back here for help. I would go with you but I need to repair some fence around the cow pasture. Our neighbor is afraid our cows will get into his corn field. Howie's dad will be out selling seed corn to our neighbors. So, you two are on your own." He pointed his finger at both boys and said again, "Be careful!"

"Okay, dad, we'll be back by 4 o'clock."

Both boys were excited, Sam more so than Howie. Sam said to himself, "This afternoon I'm going into that dark tunnel to see where it goes."

CHAPTER 10

TWO STRANGE MEN

That afternoon, after the noon meal, they started walking quickly down the lane toward the road. Sam held the giant horseshoe and Howie had the flashlight in his pocket. As the boys made their way down the lane, they noticed several cars on the road.

"That's the most cars I've ever seen on this road at one time," commented Sam.

The vehicles were moving slowly in front of the vacant farmstead. The boys could see the people in the cars looking at the buildings and pointing toward the log cabin.

"These people have read the morning newspaper. They are curious about the log cabin. After all, nothing exciting ever happens out here in the country," Sam said.

They passed through the gate and walked in the grass toward the cabin. "Watch your step, Howie," cautioned Sam.

"Okay," said Howie. He stopped abruptly. "See that car parked down there by the side of the road, Sam. Why do you think it is parked there?" he asked.

Sam stopped to look in the direction that Howie was pointing. "I don't know. The driver probably had engine trouble or a flat tire and went for help." They continued walking and soon arrived at the log cabin door.

Sam and Howie had taken only a few steps into the cabin.... when suddenly ....two men jumped up and out of the tunnel and raced toward the two windows and dived out head first.

The boys were so startled they just stood there as if their shoes were glued to the floor. Howie recovered first. He ran over to one of the windows with Sam close on his heels. They caught a glimpse of the men running toward the car parked beside the road. The men scrambled into the front seat and took off in a swirl of dust with tires squealing.

"Howie, one of those men has long red hair."

"Yeah, I saw him. Sam, this place is beginning to get on my nerves. I came here for a nice quiet visit with you, but I end up being scared to death day after day. Don't try to tell me those two guys were here to have a picnic on the grassy field. And, Sam, I'm not going down in that dark tunnel with those spiders. Why do you always insist on exploring when I come for a visit?"

Sam, however, felt his confidence coming back. "Howie, we can't quit now. We've got to get to the bottom of this mystery. I'm having more fun than I've had in years. Look, those two men think there is something in this log cabin or in the tunnel that's valuable. We need to find out what it is they're looking for. Howie, you've got to stay with me because I can't solve this mystery by myself."

Howie, feeling a little ashamed, said, "Well…okay, Sam, but you'll have to admit this log cabin, the tunnel, the skeleton and those two men are giving us a real fright."

"Good for you, Howie. That's the spirit. I knew I could count on you. Give me the flashlight and I'll go down in the dark tunnel alone. Hold on to the giant horseshoe and be on the lookout for those two strange men. If they come back, stick your head down in the hole in the floor and yell like crazy."

Sam eased himself down into the hole in the cabin floor and began to creep forward into the dark tunnel. He shivered as he passed the area where they had found the skeleton leaning up against the brick wall. So far he saw nothing but bricks, dirt, spiders and cobwebs.

He edged forward. Soon his ears began to detect noises. Yes, ….he could hear the faint sound of gurgling, running water. He crawled a little farther and soon came to the end of the tunnel, the opening hidden by trees, shrubs and weeds. He pulled apart the bushes. Now he could see and hear the bubbling creek waters that ran the length of the grassy field back of the log cabin.

He was able to squeeze his way between two of the smaller trees and jump down about five feet, splashing into the shallow, running water. Looking back, he couldn't see the entrance to the tunnel. It was well hidden by the trees and underbrush. Wading upstream for several feet he grabbed some tree roots and shrubs. He pulled himself up the creek bank to the grassy field above. Then he ran quickly back to the log cabin to tell Howie what he had found. As he entered, Howie was looking at the fireplace wall with his back to the door.

"Howie!" Sam yelled, "You won't guess what I've discovered!"

Howie was so startled he jumped and dropped the giant horseshoe.

"Where did you come from?" he demanded, as he turned to face Sam. "You just scared me half to death. I thought those two strange men had come back. How did you get out of the tunnel, Sam?"

"Easy. The tunnel ends at the creek that runs through the grassy field about 40 feet back of the cabin. The entrance to the tunnel is completely hidden by brush and trees. The floor of the tunnel is about five feet above the creek waters. That's the reason large animals couldn't get into the tunnel from the creek."

"I don't know what to think," groaned Howie. "I'm scared those two men will come back. Can we go back to the house now?"

"Stay with me, Howie. We can solve this mystery together. Let's sit down here and talk about what we know so far."

Howie hesitated, and then sat down on the floor with his back up against the log wall. "Okay, Sam, start talking," he said with a sigh.

Sam picked up the giant horseshoe from the floor and sat down next to him. He asked, "Why is this tunnel here on grandpa's farm? Why would anyone build a strong brick tunnel that leads from this log cabin to the creek?"

"Yeah, and what do those two strange men want?" chimed in Howie. "Were they after the skeleton?"

Sam ignored the question and continued, thinking out loud. "Why was the skeleton in the tunnel? How did it get there? And, how does this giant horseshoe fit into this mystery? Hey, Howie, I've got it! The skeleton is not the key to this puzzle. This giant horseshoe is."

"Wait just a minute, Sam. You mean to tell me this rusty old piece of metal is a more important clue than the skeleton? No, I don't believe it. That skeleton was a living person and it's much more important than a piece of metal. And, don't forget, the skeleton was holding the horseshoe."

"Howie, as usual, you are right. Somehow both the skeleton and this giant horseshoe hold the keys to unlock this mystery. We've got to find those keys before those two strange men find them."

CHAPTER 11

THE STONE FIREPLACE WALL

Sam looked at the giant horseshoe and turned it over and over in his hands. He thought out loud, "Why would anyone take the trouble to bend the ends of a horseshoe at right angles, especially since it was not made for a horse? And, why make the metal in the shape of a horseshoe? These marks could have been hammered on any piece of metal."

Howie, relaxing a bit, was thinking while Sam was talking. "Sam, we have a neighbor back home who nailed a horseshoe above the front door to his house. He said it was for good luck and that a lot of people believe horseshoes bring good luck to the family."

He looked up at the cabin door frame. "But this horseshoe is too big to fit above that door. There isn't enough room between the top of the door frame and the ceiling. I suppose it could have been nailed to the outside of the cabin, above the door."

He got up and went outside to look above the door frame. "There are no nail holes above the door frame on the outside. The horseshoe could have been hung inside the cabin."

Both boys began to look around the room to see if there were other places to hang a horseshoe. Sam said, "I suppose it could have been nailed in here to one of the walls."

"Well, how about the fireplace?" asked Howie.

"Howie, you are brilliant! Of course, the horseshoe should hang on the most important wall of the cabin…the stone fireplace." Sam put the horseshoe on the floor, stood up and walked over to the fireplace for a closer inspection. Both boys began to run their hands over the surface of the stones. They searched the entire fireplace wall as far up as they could reach.

THE STONE FIREPLACE WALL

"I can't reach the top, Howie. Is there something outside that I can stand on to reach farther up?"

"I saw some boards in the barn when we were exploring over there," Howie replied.

"Good, run over and bring back three or four short pieces of wood."

Howie took off and Sam continued to look at the fireplace for clues. Returning, Howie stacked the boards so Sam could reach a little higher. Sam stood on the boards and ran his hands over the stones. As he felt toward the center of the fireplace wall, he felt a small hole in one stone. As he moved his hand a little further he discovered another hole. Both holes were filled with dust.

"Howie, hand me the giant horseshoe," he said with excitement. "Let's see if it fits in these holes."

Sam placed the metal up against the stones. The bent ends fit the holes perfectly. "Howie, you're a genius! You were right! The bent ends of this piece of metal fit into these holes in the fireplace wall."

Howie smiled, feeling good that Sam recognized his intelligence.

"But," he asked, "what does that prove? So our great grandpa put a horseshoe up on the fireplace wall. That doesn't solve our mystery."

"Howie, you're right again. I was getting too excited over our discovery" Sam looked at his pocket watch. "It's almost 4 o'clock. Let's get back to the house now and talk to dad. He'll have some ideas."

As they left the log cabin with the giant horseshoe, they saw the same black car that was parked by the side of the road earlier. Both boys stopped suddenly and stared at the parked car. The two men in the car were looking very intently out the car windows in their direction.

"Hey," said Howie, "that looks like the same men who came up from the tunnel, ran and jumped out of the log cabin windows. See, one has red hair."

"Y...Yeah," stammered Sam.

The car quickly sped away. Sam and Howie were frightened. The hair on the back of their necks began to stand out straight.

"Come on!" Sam yelled. "Let's run!"

They arrived breathless at the farm shop at the same time Wilmer was putting his tools away. He had finished repairing the fence around the cow pasture. Now the neighbor could be sure Wilmer's cows would not get into his cornfield.

"Dad," Sam shouted, as he bent over with his hands on his knees, gasping for breath, "you'll never guess what we found out at the log cabin!"

"Okay, take it easy, boys. Here, both of you sit on these nail kegs and catch your breath. I'll just sit on this stool and rest myself. Well, what did you find?"

"First, when we stepped inside the log cabin, two strange men jumped up out of the tunnel, ran to the windows and jumped out head first. They ran to their car and sped away in a big hurry. We were really scared."

Then Sam explained how he explored the tunnel and found the end, facing the creek bank. "And then," he said, as he looked at Howie, "Howie had the brilliant idea that the giant horseshoe might fit on a wall in the log cabin, for good luck."

"Well, yes," murmured Wilmer, "some people believe a horseshoe does bring good luck. What else did you learn?"

"We found out the only place this horseshoe will fit on a wall in the log cabin is on the front fireplace wall. These bent ends fit perfectly two holes that have been chiseled into the stones."

Wilmer didn't say anything. He was thinking about what the boys had said.

Then Howie spoke up. "Yeah, and when we were leaving the log cabin, we saw the same two men who came up out of the tunnel and jumped out of the windows. One had red hair. They were sitting in their car and they were staring at us. We were so scared we ran all the way home."

Wilmer was quiet for a long time. Then he said, "Boys, this situation is getting serious. There is something going on here that we don't understand. We need to get more information if we're going to solve this mystery. It's too late today, but tomorrow we're going to town. We'll talk to Sheriff Neverfine again. He should be able to help us. Then we'll go to the library to see what we can find out about this area during the years my grandfather lived on that property across the road.

In the meantime, I'm going to put up some 'no trespassing' signs on the gateposts across the road. Maybe that will keep those two strangers off the property. Let's go ahead and do the evening chores. My father has invited all of us to his house for supper tonight. Perhaps he will be able to tell us more about the log cabin because he was born there in 1850. I don't remember ever hearing him say anything about his father hanging a horseshoe on that fireplace wall. He's in his 80's now, but his mind is still sharp and his memory is good. He is also a very interesting story teller."

CHAPTER 12

THE UNDERGROUND RAILROAD

That evening, everyone took a hot bath and put on clean clothes to look their best for the meal at Grandpa George's place. Sam and Howie considered wearing 'knickers' but Millie and Lenora said they should wear long pants and dress shirts. Knickers, short pants with elastic just below the knees, had been popular with boys for several years.

They piled into the two cars for the short ride to Grandpa's home, a modern, two-story house, located close to the road. It was arranged with the kitchen in the rear. The dining room connected the kitchen to the sitting room, parlor and bedrooms.

Three barns, smoke house, wood house, chicken house, two granaries, tool shed, corn cribs, root cellar, hog house and garage completed the large farmstead. The acreage and buildings were located on both sides of the road.

Grandpa George, Wilmer's father, had been born in the log cabin where Sam and Howie found the tunnel, the skeleton and the giant horseshoe. When Grandpa George married, he and his wife built this new farm home in the 1880's, up the road about a mile from the log cabin.

The ladies quickly began to prepare the mashed potatoes, green beans, fresh greens from the garden and roast beef with gravy for the evening meal. The kitchen was rather large and modern for the 1930's, with a small refrigerator, large black cook stove that used wood as fuel, pantry, preparation table, and a sink with hand pump to draw rain water from an outside, concrete tank called a cistern. Fresh water was carried in from a deep well pump located a few feet outside the kitchen door. Strips of sticky fly paper hung from the ceiling. Many dead flies dotted the paper as proof of its effectiveness.

The men, with Sam and Howie, sat on the front porch, talking and taking advantage of the gentle evening breeze. It was still very hot and everyone perspired, especially the women in the kitchen working near the wood-burning cook stove.

Finally the food was ready. Aunt Lenora, wiping her brow with her sleeve, called everyone to the table. Since Grandpa George was the head of the family, he sat at one end of the large, rectangular, wooden dining room table. Sam and Howie scooted their chairs up to one side, where they would be within easy reach of all the food. With forks in hand, they anxiously waited for the meal to begin. They leaned forward and inhaled the most wonderful aromas coming from the food that had been placed on the table. Strong black coffee was served to the adults. Milk fresh from Grandpa's cows filled the glasses in front of Sam and Howie.

Grandpa George said the 'blessing,' thanking God for the food, shelter and relatives. He asked Jesus to award good health and protection from harm and sickness. He also prayed for rain to help the parched crops. Sam thought to himself that the prayer for protection was a good prayer because of the two strange men they had seen at the log cabin. After the prayer and the "Amen," all attention was on the food, as dishes clattered, voices rose and the wooden chairs squeaked.

The dishes full of food were passed around the table. Grandpa George looked at Sam and said, "I understand you and Howie have found somethin' interesting under the old log cabin. Your dad has brought me up to date on your discoveries."

Sam had his mouth full of green beans, but he managed to nod his head.

Howie was spreading a generous coating of butter on a thick slab of home-baked bread. A large helping of home-made strawberry jam was on his plate waiting its turn to join the butter. He looked at his grandpa and bobbed his head up and down.

Grandpa George continued, talking and chewing at the same time.

"Well, Sam and Howie, I'm goin' to give you a brief history lesson about this area. First, I want to tell you about the importance of education in our family. Both my parents and my wife's parents held a high regard for schoolin'. Being educated helps us to understand what I'm goin' to tell you.

I was able to attend a one room school for six short winter terms. It was a log cabin with split logs for seats. Our desks were made of planks held up with wooden pegs driven into the wall. One teacher taught all ages. My brothers and sisters and I were all in the same room with the same teacher. Her name was Miss Learner. I remember her quite well because she was an attractive young lady with green eyes that flashed when she was angry. She was very strict and didn't hesitate to use a switch cut from a willow tree on those of us who were sleepin' or causin' trouble.

Although I had only six short terms at school, I read a lot of books and other material. Our ancestors have always insisted we get all the schoolin' and book learnin' we can. Those books you see with the Bible on the shelves in the sittin' room are books about history, mathematics and English. There are also books of poetry and science. Much of my knowledge has come from these books and from the terms at school. Also, I have gained much practical knowledge from my experiences here on this farm.

Some of what I am goin' to tell you was told to me by my relatives and friends. It was handed down from one generation to the next.... they call that folklore. But, there is a lot of truth in folklore."

All eyes were on Grandpa George. He was indeed a great storyteller.

Sam said, "Start with the tunnel, Grandpa, since that's what we discovered first."

Grandpa took another forkful of roast beef and dunked it in gravy. "That's where we will begin. First, you must realize I was born in the year 1850 in that log cabin where you boys discovered the tunnel. I came into the world just a few years before the United States Civil War began. That war was about keepin' the states together as a nation. It was also about slavery."

Howie piped up, "What's slavery, Grandpa? I've heard the word but I don't really know much about it."

"Slavery happens when a person is sold or otherwise put into bondage to another person usually against his will. A slave has very few rights and has to do what his master says. When I was born, most of the slaves in this country were negroes who lived in the southern states."

"Were there slaves in our northern states, too?" asked Sam.

"Yes," replied Grandpa, "but most were in the south. In our state of Indiana many people had strong feelings against slavery, especially some of the folks who were members of local churches."

"Sam and Howie," he continued, "what I'm goin' to tell you now is directly related to the tunnel you discovered under the log cabin."

Both boys looked at Grandpa George. They were anxious to hear more about the tunnel.

"Some of our close relatives were and are active in local churches. My Ma and Pa, who built the log cabin you are exploring, were very involved in church activities. They helped build the first church in this area. It was made of logs. Also, Ma and Pa helped set up a system to help slaves escape from the south, travel through Indiana, and other states, on their way north to Canada."

"I've read about Canada in my history books," said Sam, his mouth full of mashed potatoes. "But how does the log cabin fit into all this?"

"Now we're gettin' to the interestin' part, boys," said grandpa, as he stabbed another chunk of roast beef. "The system to help the slaves escape to Canada was called *THE UNDERGROUND RAILROAD.*"

"Wow!" exclaimed Howie. "A railroad built just for the slaves."

"No, no, Howie," corrected Grandpa, "it was not a real railroad with steam engines, tracks and rail cars. It was a network of homes and other buildin's where the runaway slaves were fed, hidden and allowed to rest on the way north."

Grandpa continued, "Before the Underground Railroad system was established, successful escapes by slaves were rare. Sometimes, the escaped slave's relatives were punished. The runaway slaves had only the North Star to guide them through unfriendly territory with mountains and forests. Problems with findin' food and shelter, and the absence of good maps were other factors that help us to understand why so few slaves arrived in Canada. This was especially true before the Underground Railroad was developed."

"Hmmmm…." said Sam out loud, as he spooned another helping of mashed potatoes onto his plate. He was thinking about what his grandpa had said.

"Pass the gravy, please, Aunt Lenora."

Grandpa George wiped his mouth on his shirt sleeve and said, "The Underground Railroad increased the number of escaped slaves who were able to reach safety. One report I read said over 50,000 slaves escaped to the north usin' the Underground Railroad system. Several hundred passed through our Grantor County."

"Wow!" said Howie.

"Now, Sam and Howie, I am goin' to tell you how your great grandparents were a part of this Underground Railroad system. My Ma and Pa decided to join with members of churches in the area to help some of the slaves as they came north through our area toward Canada. My Pa was called a 'conductor.' He led the people to his cabin and to the next stop in the system. They moved at night. The homes that were part of the system in this area were called 'stations' and were named after trees. My Pa's log cabin was called the 'Elms Station.' There were several large elm trees growing near the log cabin.

It was very important that the slaves not be caught when tryin' to get to Canada. Bounty hunters were hired by slave owners to find the runaway slaves. These hunters with their dogs were employed to track down the escaped slaves and return them to their owners. They received money for their services."

"But, Grandpa, how did the slaves know about the Underground Railroad?" asked Howie.

"I don't know for sure, but probably by word of mouth from runaway slaves who had been caught and returned to their owners."

"Okay, let's see if I understand what you have been telling us," Sam said. "A slave owned by another person decides to run away. He wants to go north to Canada where he can be free. He has heard about the Underground Railroad by word of mouth. To use this 'railroad' in this part of Indiana he goes to houses named after trees and is guided by people like my Great Grandpa, called conductors."

"Exactly, Sam," said Grandpa George loudly. "But remember, because of a law passed in 1850 by the United States congress called 'The Fugitive Slave Law,' it was against the law to help a runaway slave escape to freedom. This law was passed because land owners in the southern states, alarmed at the number of runaway slaves, put pressure on the United States congress. If my father had been caught helpin' the slaves escape he could have been put in jail for six months and forced to pay a fine of $1000."

"You mean my great grandfather was breaking the law when he helped those people escape?" Howie gasped.

"Yes, Howie, it was a very dangerous thing to do."

Sam downed another big forkful of mashed potatoes smothered with gravy. Then he asked, "But what has all of this to do with the tunnel?"

"Your great grandpa led the runaway slaves to his cabin, fed them and then hid them in the tunnel overnight and through the next day until they could be safely moved to the next home, or station, in the Underground Railroad system."

"You mean they went down through the log cabin floor and stayed in that creepy tunnel with the spiders all night? That sounds real scary to me," said Howie.

"Yep, that's what I mean. Ma and Pa would move the bed, pull the large deerskin rug to one side and open the trap door. They gave the slaves food and candles for a little light. Then they closed the trap door, replaced the rug and moved the bed back in place. If anyone came to their log cabin there was no evidence of anyone there except our family members. The next night, the slaves crawled out of the tunnel to the creek where they were led upstream to the next safe house. That way even the dogs the hunters owned could not trace them in the flowin' waters."

Sam thought about what his Grandpa had said. Then he asked, "But, Grandpa, why did your Pa build a tunnel all the way to the creek? He could have dug a hole under the cabin and lined it with bricks."

"My older brothers told me the tunnel was not only a hiding place but also an escape route to the creek. The floor of the tunnel slopes toward the creek. That way any water that collects in the tunnel will drain out. Also, the opening to the creek let in fresh air. In very bad weather the runaway slaves could get warm and be fed in the cabin before going down into the tunnel."

"Wow," said Howie, cleaning up the gravy on his plate with a crust of bread. "Imagine being in that tunnel all night with nothing but a candle. I was scared and I was in the dark tunnel only a short time."

Millie and Lenora began to clear the dishes from the table. Then they brought in two cherry pies and thick cream. "These cherries are from trees in the orchard not far from the log cabin. The trees were planted by Grandpa George's father years ago," Aunt Lenora said, as she smiled at Howie and Sam.

As everyone began to spoon in the cherry pie and cream, Grandpa George continued, "You see, boys, I was very young when this Underground Railroad was in use. My brothers and sisters and I usually went to bed shortly after sundown. We all slept in the loft above the main room, except in very cold weather. We didn't see these slaves enterin' the cabin at night and disappearin' down into the tunnel.

I heard my older brothers say something about a tunnel underneath the log cabin. They told me how the tunnel was used, but I was too young to understand the real meaning. I don't remember actually seein' the tunnel or ever bein' in the tunnel. Also, I am sure my Ma and Pa were very careful not to talk about the tunnel in front of us because we might talk to neighbors or strangers and give away the whole system. So, when I married your grandmother and built this house, I forgot all about the tunnel. That's the reason your discovery came as a surprise to most people, includin' everyone here but me."

Sam began to run the information his grandpa had given them through his mind. Now he began to understand why the tunnel was located under the log cabin. Also, he now realized why everyone was so startled when he and Howie told them about their discovery.

"But, wait a minute," Sam blurted out. "That explains the tunnel, but what about the skeleton and the giant horseshoe?"

"Let's move to the sittin' room and let the ladies clear the rest of these dishes," said Grandpa George, as he grabbed two canes that were leaning against the table.

He required these two canes to support himself when moving about the house. Wilmer had told Sam his father had stepped on some rusted metal years ago while walking behind a plow pulled by a team of horses. The wound did not heal and the injury resulted in blood poisoning. The leg was cut off below the knee in an operation performed at home on the very dining table we had used for the evening meal. His artificial leg and foot, custom made of leather and wood, squeaked with every step as he made his way into the sitting room.

The gentle evening breeze flowed through the tall, open windows of the sitting room and swayed the floor-length lace curtains to and fro. The wallpaper had a bold, distinct pattern of large red and purple flowers. The side of the room opposite the windows was dominated by a large heating stove with isinglass panels, making the flames visible to the people sitting in the room. Of course, the stove was now cold, not used since the April chill.

On the walls were photographs and portraits of family members and ancestors. Two Maxfield Parrish paintings decorated the wall next to the bookcase. A few pieces of Carnival Glass rested on the library table. A wind-up clock ticked loudly on the wall above the table.

Next to the clock hung a framed message from the Bible; 2 Peter: Chapter 1, verse 3: 'We have everything we need to live a life that pleases God.' It had been written in fancy letters by Lenora when she was 8 years old. She used her own words to capture the meaning of the verse.

They settled in chairs and rockers as Grandpa George continued,

"I can't help you with the skeleton, boys. I have no idea how or why it ended up in the tunnel."

Wilmer broke in, "It could be the remains of a slave who died in the tunnel."

Uncle Francis thought a moment, then said, "A possibility, I suppose, but unless the slave was sick, he could have crawled out through the exit to the creek."

"Yes, I guess you're right, Francis," said Wilmer. "Also, over the many years small animals would have disturbed the bones. I think the skeleton is of more recent origin."

Wilmer continued, "The Indiana State Police report should answer some of our questions about the skeleton. I'm afraid the answers are going to be disturbing."

"Yes, Wilmer, disturbin' is the right word," said Grandpa George. "Anytime an unidentified skeleton is found, a mystery lurks until the puzzle is solved. I'm glad the state police are workin' the case."

At this point, the ladies joined the group and entered into the discussion. Lenora spoke up. "What do you think of all these events, father? The boys have been driving Millie and me crazy with their stories. Since that farm has been in our family for years, finding a skeleton in a tunnel under the log cabin is very alarming."

"Yes, indeed it is," replied Grandpa. "And we all need to work together to solve this mystery. We need to scratch our heads and think back to see if we can remember any clues that might help us reach a solution."

Sam broke in and asked, "Grandpa, what about the horseshoe?"

"Oh, yes. The giant horseshoe, as you have called it. This, too, is quite disturbin' because you found it with the bones of the skeleton. Wilmer has told me about you being able to fit the bent ends of the horseshoe into the fireplace wall. I don't remember ever seeing a horseshoe hanging on the fireplace wall, or anywhere else inside or outside the log cabin."

Grandpa continued, "I've heard many of my relatives say that some people think the horseshoe has mysterious powers. Also, I've read in those books on the shelves behind you about horseshoes and the good luck they are supposed to bring their owners."

"Does the horseshoe really bring good luck, Grandpa?" asked Sam.

"In my opinion, no," he replied. "The belief that the horseshoe brings good luck and protects its owner goes back centuries. Iron, the metal from which horseshoes are made, was once thought to have protective qualities."

"Go on, Grandpa, this is interesting stuff," said Howie.

"Well," he continued, "many years ago people tried to protect the hooves of horses by fastenin' fabric, wood or leather to the bottom of the hoof. When the blacksmith made the shoe out of iron, the solution was found."

"Has the blacksmith always been the person to put the shoes on the horses?" asked Sam.

"Yes, the blacksmith always has been held in high regard among the tradesmen because of his ability to work with iron."

"So why did a blacksmith make a horseshoe as large as the one we found with the skeleton?" asked Sam.

"That I don't know," responded Grandpa, with a serious look on his face. "It has some important meaning, especially with those marks on the surface. I hope you boys get to the bottom of this mystery. I'm very anxious for you to find a solution because you found the skeleton and the giant horseshoe on our property."

The clock on the wall chimed 9 o'clock. Grandpa was beginning to yawn. Wilmer and Francis took that as a cue they should leave. The men complimented the ladies on the delightful and tasty supper. Everyone rose from their chairs and said their goodbyes. Wilmer and Francis and their families piled into the cars and headed for home.

All were quiet, thinking about the information provided by Grandpa George and the discussions around the dining table and in the sitting room. Sam looked at Howie and broke the silence. "I'm excited. We've got to think and think hard if we are going to solve this mystery. You're still with me aren't you, Howie?"

"Yeah, I'm still with you, but right now I'm too sleepy to think about any skeleton or horseshoe."

As soon as they arrived home, the boys ran upstairs, dropped their clothes on the floor, put on their striped pajamas and jumped in bed. They were excited about seeing Sheriff Neverfine the next day. Sam was thinking to himself, "The sheriff, Howie and I will solve this mystery. We're getting closer. All we need is more information about the skeleton and the giant horseshoe. But.... what do those two strange men want?"

CHAPTER 13

SAM AND HOWIE IN JAIL

The next morning Sam and Howie joined Wilmer in the family car for the trip to Manion to talk to Sheriff Neverfine. The boys were quiet for a long time looking out the windows at the passing fields of corn and alfalfa pasture.

They passed the Katchnot home where the burglary had taken place a few days ago. Seeing the house brought back memories of the stranger with red hair. Sam shuddered.

Then he asked, "Dad, are there any people living around here now who go to the same church that Grandpa George attended?"

"Oh yes," replied Wilmer. "There are four or five families living within a few miles of our home that go to the same church. The Hardings live south of us a mile and, the Softners live about a half mile east. Both families have been farmers in the area for years. It's possible that their ancestors were also part of the Underground Railroad system."

"How many of our relatives went to the same church as Grandpa George when he lived in the log cabin?" asked Sam.

"Almost all the folks on my mother's side of the family were members of the same church. Their last name is Bendbranch. They lived three miles south of us on a small farm. My mother was a Bendbranch before she married George, my father."

"Then, why aren't we going to that church?"

Wilmer began to explain. "Back two generations ago travel was very difficult in this part of the country because of the dense forests and the lack of roads. At first Indian trails were used for transportation. Everyone traveled by walking, riding a horse, or riding in a wagon or buggy pulled by animals. People went to the church that was closest to their homes. My mother's parents, the Bendbranches, walked a mile to church carrying their young daughter, who years later became your Grandpa's wife."

Wilmer added, "The Lugar Creek Chapel was closer to Grandpa George's home than the other churches, so that is where most of our family attended church. The old Lugar Creek Church was destroyed by fire. It was rebuilt and that is where we go to church today."

"It's amazing that Grandpa George's mother and father actually helped those people escape to Canada and weren't arrested and put in jail," said Sam.

"Yes, my grandfather and grandmother were very brave people who believed they should help the runaway slaves. Well, here we are on the outskirts of the town."

About 25,000 people lived in Manion, the nearest town to The HayBend Farm, where people did their banking and shopping. Many people worked in the factories scattered around the town.

They passed an empty field at the edge of town where a circus was held each spring. Wilmer pointed to the field and explained, "When the circus comes to town, the animals, work crews and performers all arrive by train. After unloading, they parade down this very road with a marching band to the circus grounds. I've always enjoyed watching the elephants pull on the ropes to erect the Big Top tents."

At the railroad crossing just east of the town center, they were stopped by flashing lights, ringing bells and a gate that was lowered whenever a train was passing through.

"Boys, watch what happens when the station master climbs down that ladder. His office is located in the shack up there on the platform by the railroad tracks."

Sam and Howie leaned out the car windows to watch. As the freight train rumbled past, the engineer in the locomotive held out his arm and snagged a note tied to a loop of string. The string was stretched across the ends of the arms of a Y-shaped stick. The station master held the stick up so the engineer could put his arm through the loop of string as the train roared by.

"That's the way he gives the engineer messages without having the train stop," said Wilmer.

Sam and Howie were fascinated by what they had just seen. "I wonder what would happen if the string broke," said Howie.

"Then the engineer wouldn't get the message," replied Sam, with a smirk.

Howie poked him in the ribs. "Let's count the cars," he said.

After several minutes the caboose appeared and the protective arm swung up and away. "Well, how many freight cars did you count?" asked Wilmer, as he drove across the tracks and continued toward Sheriff Neverfine's office.

"Sixty-two, after we started counting," replied Howie. Sam agreed the number was correct.

As Wilmer drove toward the county jail, they passed an Oldsmobile sales agency and an Indian motorcycle dealership. At the town center there were theatres, stores and many places of business. Wilmer and Millie bought most of their clothes and shoes at the R. U. Ready store, located on the public square, across the street from the courthouse. This store had oiled wood floors that creaked as you walked on them. Slow moving fans suspended from the ceiling circulated the hot summer air.

When a purchase was made, the package was wrapped in brown paper torn from a large roll by the clerk and tied with string. All money for purchases was sent to a person who was seated in a booth on a balcony at the rear of the store. That person sent any change due the customer back to the sales clerk. A system of vacuum tubes moved the money back and forth in small, round, cylinder-shaped containers. Sam was always amazed by the system for handling money. Fence, hardware, and other farm supplies were purchased at other stores in Manion or in other villages near their home.

Most of the food for the table was produced on the farm but Millie bought sugar, coffee, flour and other food items at a small grocery store located directly across the street from the jail. Usually, she would take eggs she had collected on the farm to the store and trade them for groceries. Mr. Markup, the grocer, would count the eggs and give Millie the money for them, and she would buy the few items she needed. Sam always asked his mother to buy a few bananas, a luxury food at the HayBend Farm.

"Well, here we are at the jail where the sheriff's office is located," said Wilmer. "He and his family live on the first floor."

Sam had been past the jail many times as his family came to town to do the weekly shopping. However, he had not paid much attention to the building, but today he and Howie were all eyes and ears as Wilmer parked the car by the curb in front of the jail.

The jail looked like a castle from the outside. Built of Indiana limestone, brick, concrete and steel, it was located in downtown Manion. Several large trees grew on the lawn in front of the jail. The building was four floors high and looked like a picture out of the English countryside. Sam and Howie had seen such pictures in their history books.

They climbed the stone steps to the jail and walked directly to the sheriff's office. "Good morning," said the sheriff, smiling as he sipped a mug of steaming hot coffee. "I'm glad you came in to see me today. You'll want to see what the Indiana State Police put in their report about the skeleton you found in the tunnel under the log cabin. But, before we talk, I've got time to show you around. If these two boys see the inside of a jail, they'll never want to be a guest here," he said, smiling and chuckling as he looked at Sam and Howie. He motioned for them to follow.

"The only wood used in the construction of this jail is found on the first floor where we live. That's to prevent the prisoners from setting fire to the building," began the sheriff. "The walls are 18 inches thick and that makes it difficult for a prisoner to escape from here. That apartment over there is for the jailer and his family. They prepare all the food for the prisoners. In the back of the jail there is a playground for our children."

SHERIFF NEVERFINE

On the second floor Sam and Howie noticed a large room in the center that looked like a cage with iron bars. "This is what we call the Bull Pen. Here the prisoners are given free time away from their cells. They can receive visitors and family members on Sundays. They can talk through the bars to people on the outside of the bull pen as the jailer watches."

They walked on and met the wife of the jailer, Mrs. Stewless. She greeted them and said, "Yes, I am the cook for the prisoners. I prepare beans with salt pork every day for them. We usually add boiled potatoes and corn. On Sunday we add meat to the meal. Each prisoner is given seven slices of bread at noon and that is to last until the next noon meal. Coffee and water are always available." Sam was comparing the daily ration of seven slices of bread to the number of slices he ate each day as they walked on.

Sam and Howie just stared with their mouths open as they were led to the section where the prisoners were kept in their cells. They wore faded, black and white striped uniforms. Most of them were napping or reading. The cells were about six feet by twelve feet with metal bunks, a sink and a toilet. The prisoners just looked and frowned at the boys as they passed by.

The boys were very quiet as they returned to the first floor. The sheriff directed them to his office and motioned for them to sit on some old wooden chairs. As Sam and Howie sat down, they were in deep thought. They were still numb from what they had just seen. The sheriff's office was very plain with vertical wooden boards for walls. A hat rack, made from wooden pegs, stretched across the wall back of the sheriff's desk. A rifle was mounted above the hat rack. A telephone and coffee cup, usually empty, were the only items found on the top of the old wood desk.

The sheriff lowered his large bulk into a large wooden chair with armrests. Scooting the chair up to his desk and clearing his throat, he reached in the top drawer and pulled out a thick document of several pages. "I have the Indiana State Police report right here. I think it answers some questions, but opens up other areas that must be investigated."

Sam and Howie squirmed in their chairs, anxious to hear what the sheriff was going to say next.

"First," he said, "the report says the skeleton belongs to a white male about 45 years old. Also, the skeleton has been in the tunnel for at least 10 years."

"So," said Wilmer, looking at Sam and Howie, "that means it was not a runaway slave who died in the tunnel years ago."

"That is correct," said the sheriff. "I remember you told me the log cabin was a part of the Underground Railroad system in the mid 1800's. This skeleton does not date back to that period."

Sam and Howie were too excited to say anything. They looked at each other, then at the sheriff, expecting him to explain more about the report.

Wilmer asked, "Does the report indicate the cause of death?"

"Yes it does," answered sheriff Neverfine, lifting his eyebrows. "Some of the bone tissue was tested. The state police laboratory report says the man died of an unknown poison. Folks, I could have an unsolved murder on my hands."

"Wow!" yelled Howie, "A murder!" Now his mind was racing as fast as Sam's. "He had the giant horseshoe in his hand and died in the tunnel because someone murdered him. Why?"

Before the sheriff could answer Howie, Sam jumped in. "Is there a connection between the giant horseshoe and this murder? And, why would anyone resort to murder because of a horseshoe?"

"Wait a minute. Wait a minute. Don't jump to conclusions. I said I could have a murder on my hands!" yelled the sheriff in a loud voice.

Then, in a quieter tone, he said, "I remember Wilmer saying something about a giant horseshoe, but I don't think there is any connection between the skeleton and the horseshoe. That would stretch my imagination beyond belief." The sheriff then scooted back and lifted his large frame from his chair, giving everyone the impression the meeting was over.

"That's about it for now. I may want to talk to all of you at a later time. I appreciate you coming in today. Keep me informed of any developments. We need to work together to solve this mystery."

As Wilmer and the boys left the jail not a word was spoken. They were in deep thought about what the sheriff had said. Wilmer looked at his pocket watch. "Oh, oh, it's too late to go to the library today. It closes at noon."

As they walked to the car, Sam was very quiet, thinking about the sheriff's suggestion that the skeleton might be the result of a murder. Then he thought about their close call with the two strange men. He shuddered.

CHAPTER 14

WHAT DO THE CLUES MEAN?

After they were seated in the car and on their way home, Wilmer spoke up. "You boys really stumbled on to something when you discovered that tunnel and skeleton. At first I thought you were just on another of your wild exploring adventures. Now, I'm ready to help you solve this mystery. When we get home, why don't you go over to the log cabin this afternoon and see if you can get some ideas about the meaning of those markings on the giant horseshoe?"

"Yeah!" cried both boys, in the same breath.

"This afternoon," said Sam eagerly, "we'll take the giant horseshoe and put it in the holes in the fireplace wall. Then we'll try to figure out what those markings mean."

"By the way, Sam, where is the horseshoe?" asked Howie.

"I hid it in the farm shop on the top shelf behind a sack of seed corn Uncle Francis sold to dad. I didn't want to take it to the sheriff's office, and I didn't want to leave it out in plain sight while we were away."

"Smart thinking, Sam," said Howie, as he slapped him on the shoulder.

Wilmer turned onto the farm lane and they soon pulled up to the rear porch entrance to the house. As they entered the kitchen, they found Uncle Francis, Aunt Lenora and Millie drinking iced tea. They were busily talking around the dining table.

Millie, visibly shaken and fingering an empty iced tea glass, looked up and spoke first. "I'm so glad you're back," she said. "While you were in town, two strange men drove up to the house and knocked on the porch door. When I answered, one of the men said they wanted to buy any antiques we might have for sale."

"Yes," Uncle Francis added, "we could all hear the conversation. Millie let them in to the back porch."

"We noticed they were always leaning around the door frame and looking to see what was in the kitchen," added Aunt Lenora.

Millie continued, "They said they were especially interested in old items related to horses, such as saddles, harness, bridles, and horseshoes."

"They wanted horseshoes?" Sam yelled. "What did those men look like?"

"Well, let's see now," thought Millie, as she fiddled with her apron, twisting it with both hands. "They were of average height, one a little taller than the other. One had long red hair and was a muscular man with a large chest."

"And, the other man," added Lenora, "had dark hair and was of slight build."

Uncle Francis piped up, "I've talked to a lot of people in my day, and there is something strange about those two. I can't put my finger on it, but I wouldn't trust them one little bit."

At last, Sam could jump into the conversation. "I'll bet those men are the same two scary men Howie and I saw in and around the cabin," he shouted. "They are the men who dived out the log cabin windows. They are the ones who have been scaring us half to death. Howie, those men are up to no good."

"You're right, Sam. I had nightmares last night about those two. Say, Aunt Millie, did those men go out around any of the other farm buildings?"

Before Millie could answer, Sam took off like a shot, running at top speed toward the farm shop to see if the horseshoe was still hidden behind the sack of seed corn. With great relief, Sam found the giant horseshoe and brought it back to the kitchen. Sam was still breathing hard as he said, "The tunnel, the skeleton, this horseshoe and those two strange men are all part of this mystery. Howie, we have got to find the answer before they do!"

Howie and Sam were so excited they could hardly eat the peanut butter and jelly sandwiches served at the noon meal. They bolted down a glass of lemonade, grabbed the giant horseshoe and ran out the porch, slamming the door behind them.

They were out the door when Howie stopped Sam and said, "Wait a minute, let's take along the piece of paper with the diagrams of the markings. It's easier for us to see the markings on paper."

"Yeah," replied Sam, "that's a good idea. Go back up to my room and get it. It's on the table by the bed."

Howie ran back through the kitchen, clambered up the stairs two steps at a time and grabbed the paper. He raced back down the stairs, stumbled on the last step and sprawled headlong on the dining room floor with his head ending up under the china closet. Picking himself up, he ran through the kitchen and porch and was soon out at Sam's side.

As Howie slammed the porch door, Millie shouted out the kitchen window, "You boys be careful. Be back here by 4 o'clock."

"Howie, you look a little shook up," said Sam.

"Yeah, I tripped coming down the stairs and took a slider clear across the dining room floor."

Sam looked at Howie and laughed.

They walked rapidly down the lane.

"Will we need the flashlight, Sam?" asked Howie.

"I don't think so since we aren't going down into the dark tunnel."

They approached the log cabin and walked around the building to make sure they were alone. Sam entered the door with Howie close on his heels, eyes wide with anticipation. "Howie, I'm going to put the giant horseshoe on the fireplace wall so it fits into those holes chiseled in the stones."

"The wood I brought from the barn is still here, Sam. Stand on top so you can reach all the way up to the stones with the holes."

Sam stood on the wood with the horseshoe in one hand. He ran his other hand over the surface of the stones until he felt the holes. He then placed the giant horseshoe on the fireplace wall. "There," he said, "that is the way it is supposed to hang, right in the center, with the curved part on top."

Then, both boys stood back and stared at the horseshoe trying to understand the meaning of the markings on the surface, especially the star with four points.

Howie was the first to speak. "When we drew stars for our art teacher at school last year, she made us put five points on each one. Since this star has four points, the number four could have a special meaning."

"Howie, again, you're thinking straight."

"Sam, I think the star with four points and the arrow pointing down means four times 'something' in a down direction."

"Howie, look at our diagram on this paper. The next mark on the giant horseshoe is the small figure that looks like a fireplace."

"Yeah, Sam," said Howie excitedly. "As we look at the fireplace, what could that 'something' be?"

Sam replied, "Stones are the only thing below the horseshoe."

"That's it, Sam!" said Howie, bursting with excitement. "Count down four stones and you come to this round stone here."

"But, it looks ordinary to me," he continued, in a quiet voice.

"Sam, look on our diagram. Below the mark of the fireplace is an arrow pointing to our right."

"Yeah, Howie, and then there's the star with five points."

Howie was excited. "Sam, count five stones to the right."

Sliding his hands over the surface of the stones, Sam counted from one to five. The fifth stone was larger than the others, and the mortar around the stone was of a lighter color. Sam and Howie stood back and looked at the stone for a long time.

Finally Sam said, "Howie, there are no more arrows on the giant horseshoe. This mark in the shape of a rectangle must represent that stone."

"But that stone isn't shaped like a rectangle," said Howie. "It looks more like the side of a loaf of bread."

"Yeah, you're right," said Sam with a sad tone in his voice. "I thought we were headed in the right direction. I just don't know what to think of this mystery. I'm stumped. Maybe dad was right when he said these markings on the giant horseshoe probably don't mean a thing."

Sam and Howie were very disappointed they could not come up with an answer to all the mysterious markings on the giant horseshoe.

"Sam, what time is it?"

"It's almost 4 o'clock. We need to get back to the house. Well ,Howie, it looks like our adventure is over. I guess these marks on the horseshoe aren't clues after all. Maybe a blacksmith did make this horseshoe as a sign to advertise his shop. But, I'm going to take the giant horseshoe back to the house and keep it in my room as a souvenir," added Sam, as he moved toward the fireplace wall to retrieve the horseshoe.

At that moment… two heads suddenly popped up from the hole in the cabin floor.

The one with red hair yelled, "Grab the horseshoe, Sly! Don't let those two brats have it."

"Yowie!!!" yelled Howie and Sam at same time. "Yowie!!! It's them. It's them. Yowie!!!"

SLY AND SLICK

CHAPTER 15

SLY AND SLICK

Both men jumped up and out of the hole in the cabin floor and rushed toward the boys. Sly lurched forward and pushed his nose within inches of Sam's face. He threw up his arms, shaking them in a threatening way and growled in a loud and angry voice. The red haired man met Howie face to face. He stooped down, scowled, yelled and shook his fists in the air near Howie's eyes.

"Yowie!" yelled both boys again. Their eyes bulged out and their hair stood on end. They were so scared they stood frozen in place.

Then, the men raced past Sam and Howie toward the fireplace wall. The red headed man shouted, "Thanks, boys, for solving the mystery of the markings on the horseshoe for us."

Sly grabbed the horseshoe off the fireplace wall. Then both men ran to the windows, dived out, turned somersaults on the grass, and sprinted toward the road. Sam and Howie finally realized what was happening and ran to the windows, only to see a black car speeding away down the road.

Howie was still shaking as he said in a quivering voice, "S..S…S…, Sam, those men must have heard everything we said. N…N…Now they know about the marks on the giant horseshoe."

"Y..Y..Yeah, and they know what we think some of the marks mean," replied Sam, as he leaned against the log cabin wall, his knees weak and knocking together.

"B..But, Sam, if they heard us talking about the markings, and they know we're at a dead end, why did they take the giant horseshoe?"

"There are still two more marks on the horseshoe that are a mystery to us. We don't know the meaning of the rectangle or the star with eight points. There could be a connection between that fireplace stone and the mark of a rectangle. They thought if we kept the horseshoe we might be able to solve this mystery. If they have it, they think they can figure out the answer."

"And," Howie added, "if they find the answer to the last two markings they will solve this mystery before we do."

"We can't let them do that, Howie," Sam replied, with a renewed interest in the mystery. "We have to go back home. It's after 4 o'clock now. Let's talk to dad. Maybe he will have some ideas. Come on; let's get out of here before those men come back."

"Do you still have the paper diagram of the horseshoe markings?"

"Yep, right here in my pocket."

"Good, those two men don't know we have a paper copy of the horseshoe markings. Let's go."

They ran as fast as they could through the grassy field, scattering several cows on the way. They closed the gate, raced across the road, ran pell-mell up the lane, and bolted through the door in the farm shop. Wilmer was sharpening a sickle he had used for cutting weeds around the barn.

As they rushed headlong and breathless into the farm shop, Wilmer looked up, and with alarm asked, "What's the trouble, boys?"

"Dad, we think we know what four of the markings on the horseshoe mean. But, we can't figure out the other two."

"Then," Howie blurted out, "those same two strange men, one with red hair, jumped up out of the tunnel, ran over to the fireplace wall and grabbed the giant horseshoe. They threatened both of us as they ran past us to get the horseshoe."

"Yeah," Sam added, "then they jumped out of the cabin windows, ran to their car and away they went."

"Did those men harm either of you two boys?" asked Wilmer, with his eyebrows raised and his voice stern.

Both boys shook their heads. "No, but they sure scared us half to death," said Howie, still shaking inside.

"So," Wilmer continued, as he placed the sharpened sickle on the workbench, "the two men were down in the tunnel while you talked about the horseshoe markings. You talked about knowing what the first four marks mean, but you couldn't figure out the last two marks. You were ready to leave and take the horseshoe with you. At that point, the two men jumped up and out of the tunnel, threatened you, took the horseshoe, leaped out the log cabin windows, ran to their car and drove off."

"Yep, that's the way it happened," said Sam, still breathing hard.

Wilmer, almost talking to himself, said, "That means those two men think the horseshoe markings are valuable clues in this mystery. When they determine the meaning of the last two marks they will have the solution. They must think the solution represents something very valuable."

"What'll we do, dad?" Sam asked. "We can't let them beat us to the meaning of those last two marks."

"I think you're right, son, especially since the stone fireplace is on Grandpa George's property. It's a little late today, but tomorrow morning I'll go with you to the log cabin. We'll try to come up with some answers."

"Okay, dad, we think one of the stones in the fireplace wall might hold the key to this mystery."

Wilmer replied, "We'll take along some tools in case we want to remove stones from the fireplace wall. Now, let's do the evening chores and get to the house for supper. At that time we can tell everybody what you have learned."

That evening at the supper table all the conversation was about the mysterious markings on the giant horseshoe. There was a lot of concern for the boy's safety because of the two strange men who threatened Sam and Howie and stole the horseshoe from the fireplace wall.

After a period of silence, Millie said, "Wilmer, I'm worried about Sam and Howie. They've had two unpleasant and dangerous contacts with those two strange men, who have threatened and frightened them. Those men know something about the giant horseshoe or they wouldn't be interested in stealing it. They could harm our boys or hold them for ransom, or do some other evil deed."

"I'm concerned too, Millie," replied Wilmer, in a calm voice. "But look at it this way. Since they don't know the meaning of the last two marks on the horseshoe, they may wait for us to solve the mystery for them. Then they will try to steal whatever valuable items are found. They probably won't harm us until we completely solve the puzzle. Remember, dear, this whole thing could be a wild goose chase."

"I think Millie's concern is justified," said Uncle Francis, in a serious tone. "These boys must have one of us with them at all times while they are at the log cabin."

"Perhaps you're right, Francis," replied Wilmer, with some relief. "Why don't you join the boys and me tomorrow when we go over to investigate the stones on the fireplace wall."

Everyone seemed to be satisfied with the plan for the next day. They relaxed and enjoyed the sauerkraut, mashed potatoes, cold roast beef, and fresh beets from the garden. Fresh peach pie, another one of Sam's favorites, was served for dessert.

That night Sam tossed and turned as he tried to sleep. He kept seeing the angry, scowling faces of the two strange men who had scared the wits out of them at the log cabin earlier in the day. Also, his mind continued to focus on the last two marks on the giant horseshoe. "Those two marks are a part of this mystery. Tomorrow," he told himself, "we are going to find the answer."

CHAPTER 16

THE COPPER BOX

The next morning Millie and Aunt Lenora cooked a tasty breakfast of scrambled eggs and ham. Sam and Howie ate their fill and excused themselves from the table.

Sam stuffed the paper diagram with the markings in his pocket. Howie found the flashlight. They joined Wilmer and Uncle Francis for the brisk walk to the log cabin. Wilmer brought along a hammer, chisel, and pry bar in case they wanted to remove stones from the fireplace. Several cows looked at them and mooed.

"Sam, you stepped right in it," said Howie, as they walked toward the log cabin. He smiled broadly as he watched Sam wipe his shoes on the grass. They entered the cabin and walked directly to the fireplace.

Wilmer looked at Howie and said, "Let me have the flashlight a minute. We don't want those two men surprising us today." He took the flashlight over to the hole in the floor. He jumped down into the hole and pointed the light down the tunnel. When he was sure no one was there, he returned to the room above.

Uncle Francis asked, "Which stone is the one indicated by the first four markings on the giant horseshoe?"

"This one right here," said both Sam and Howie, as they pointed to the large stone surrounded by the lighter colored mortar.

"Well, it looks innocent enough," said Wilmer. "Let's see if we can get it out of the fireplace wall."

They took turns with the hammer and chisel, chipping at the mortar holding the stone in place. After an hour's work most of the surrounding mortar had been chipped away and the stone began to move.

"Here, Francis," suggested Wilmer, "use the pry bar. See if you can coax it out of the wall."

They continued prying and chiseling for several more minutes, trying to edge the stone out of its resting place. Then, suddenly, it fell out on the log cabin floor with a thud.

"Howie, hand me the flashlight," said Wilmer. "We'll see if there is anything in there." He directed the light into the opening. Sam and Howie stood on their tiptoes and strained to see any object that might be hidden in the back of the hole.

"There is something in there!" yelled everyone at once.

"Take it easy now," cautioned Uncle Francis. "Be careful putting your hands in there."

"Let's see if we can coax it out with the pry bar," suggested Wilmer.

Sam and Howie were speechless. Could this be another dead end with more disappointment? Or, have they found the meaning of the last two markings on the giant horseshoe?

All eyes were focused on the hole in the fireplace wall.

"It's some kind of a box!" exclaimed Wilmer loudly.

"Here it comes, easy now," urged Francis.

Soon Wilmer and Francis were able to grasp the edges of the metal box and pull it out of the hole. They carefully set it down on the floor. The container looked like it had been in the stone fireplace wall for many years. The log cabin was very quiet as everyone looked with amazement at the container, about the size of a loaf of bread.

Suddenly, Howie sneezed loudly. Francis, Wilmer and Sam all looked at him and frowned. He ducked behind Francis as he blew his nose.

"It seems to be made of copper, and it has a lid," said Wilmer, as he picked up the box, scraped a layer of dust off the top with the pry bar, and examined it. "Shall we go ahead and try to open it?"

Uncle Francis replied, raising his voice, "I think it might be a good idea to let Sheriff Neverfine open the box. That way he can make a list of the contents, and even take pictures. If the box is empty, he can record that information also."

"You're right. That's a good idea," said Wilmer, with some relief. "That way, if the box is empty, no one can say we took anything from it before we took it to the sheriff's office. We can take it in this afternoon."

Although they were disappointed at not knowing if the box contained any valuable items, Sam and Howie thought the adults probably knew the best way to proceed.

"At least, Howie, this afternoon we'll know what's in the box."

"But, Sam, what if it's empty?"

"Then we'll know that this whole adventure is a big joke, and the joke will be on us."

"Not so fast, Sam," cautioned Howie. "We now know the rectangle mark on the giant horseshoe refers to this copper box. But what about the mark that looks like a star with eight points?"

"Oh, yeah," confessed Sam. "I don't know. I forgot all about the last mark on the horseshoe. Thanks, Howie, for reminding me. I told you we need each other to solve this mystery."

After making sure there was nothing else in the hole in the fireplace wall, Wilmer replaced the stone. As he stepped back and looked at the fireplace wall, he now understood why all the marks were made on the right hand side of the giant horseshoe. The copper container was found behind a stone on the right side of the fireplace.

"Okay, let's go," he said. "I'm anxious to see what's inside this box."

Millie and Lenora had the noon meal ready when they returned home. Sam and Howie piled their plates high with potato salad, baked beans, lettuce from the garden with vinegar and cold, baked ham. The conversation was lively as everyone tried to guess the contents of the copper box. Even Uncle Francis, Aunt Lenora and Millie gave their opinions. All thought the box contained items that were valuable.

Sam and Howie were curious. After the noon meal, they picked up the box and turned it over and over as they brought the box up to their ears. But they could hear no movement inside. They would have to wait for the sheriff to open it. Then they would know if it contained diamonds and precious stones, or maybe even gold and silver coins. Then the disturbing thought crossed their minds. Perhaps the box is empty.

CHAPTER 17

THE CONTENTS REVEALED

When Wilmer, Francis, Sam and Howie arrived at Sheriff Neverfine's office in the jail that afternoon, he was taking a hand-cuffed prisoner to his cell. When he returned he was carrying a large iron ring with keys to the jail cells. He dropped them in a desk drawer and motioned for all to enter his office. He greeted everyone, carried chairs from the hallway and invited everyone to sit down. "I wasn't expecting you today," he said. "What's up?"

Uncle Francis was introduced to the sheriff. Soon the conversation changed from the hot weather to serious questions about the giant horseshoe. Wilmer brought the sheriff up to date on the meaning of the markings on the horseshoe, except the one that looked like a star with eight points.

Wilmer added, "Sam and Howie here figured out the meanings of the first four marks on the giant horseshoe. These four markings are clues that led them to a certain stone in the fireplace wall. They discovered the rectangle mark on the giant horseshoe refers to that stone. We are proud of them for figuring this out."

Sam and Howie, looking at each other, sat up straight in their chairs and smiled.

The sheriff squirmed about in his chair, sighed and tried to listen politely. He didn't seem to be impressed. He was slightly annoyed that his daily routine was being interrupted.

"And, we removed that stone from the fireplace wall," Wilmer continued. "Behind the stone we found this container. We decided to wait and ask you to open it so that the contents, if any, can be recorded." He placed the box on the desk in front of the sheriff.

Sheriff Neverfine pushed his wire-rimmed eye glasses up on his nose, frowned and firmed his lips as he looked at the box. He thought to himself, "How is examining this old box an important part of my law enforcement duties here in Grantor County? Someone could be robbing a bank down the street and I'm here in the jail looking at an old tarnished box two kids have found in a broken-down log cabin. What will these two boys think of next?"

He was interested, but suspicious. He was a little upset that two young country boys could make him, a long-time sheriff and respected law man spend his valuable time examining a box found on a farm in an old log cabin. He looked at it for a long time as he tapped his fingers on the desk top. He was thinking... "How could a box found in an abandoned log cabin be of any value? It was surely empty. But, it did seem to be made of copper. The lid does come down over the bottom part and it does not have hinges or a fastener. It could contain something valuable...but I doubt it. But...it could..."

Finally, curiosity got the best of him.

"Well, okay, let's take it over to my workbench and see if we can get the lid to come off," said the sheriff with a sigh, as he grabbed the copper box and rose from his chair with little enthusiasm. They all followed him to another room where he clamped the copper box in a vise on a work table. One bare light bulb dangled from the ceiling over the center of the table. He then took a hammer and a screwdriver and began to tap at the edge of the lid, trying to force it up and off the lower part. After a few minutes of tapping and prying, the lid began to move up. All heads were leaning over the table and all eyes were on the box.

No one spoke a word.

Then, suddenly, the lid popped off and landed on the floor. All five people were standing and straining forward over the table to get a glimpse of the contents.

Sam yelled out, "There is something in there!"

Suddenly, Sheriff Neverfine forgot about his plans for the afternoon and became more interested in the copper box. He bent over, pushed his glasses up on his nose and focused his attention on the contents.

Then the room was very quiet. Everyone was breathing heavily, especially the sheriff.

Without speaking, Sheriff Neverfine took a pair of tongs and gently lifted an object, wrapped in cloth, out of the box and gingerly placed it on some newspaper lying on the table. Using the tongs, he began to carefully remove the cloth wrapping from the object.

No one uttered a word as all their attention was riveted on the object.

Then Howie sneezed loudly. Everyone jumped. The sheriff gave him a stern look over his wire rimmed glasses, frowned, and cleared his throat. Howie ducked behind Francis.

As the sheriff removed the last layer of cloth, exposing the object to light from the bulb overhead, everyone crowded forward to get a better view. Then their jaws dropped as they gasped with amazement. The object looked like a large medal of some kind with eight points coming out from a center point like a star. Mounted on the center was a large, green gemstone set against a background of red and black. The gemstone reflected light in a dazzling way. Everyone around the table just stared in awe at the object, speechless.

"Well, I'll declare!" said the sheriff with disbelief, breaking the silence.

"I'll be plague gone!" said Uncle Francis, loudly.

"Jumpin' Lizards!" Wilmer yelled, with uncommon enthusiasm.

Howie, with his hands in his pockets, was quiet.

"What is it?" asked Sam.

It was then very quiet in the room, so when the sheriff belched everyone was startled.

Sam spoke again, asking in a louder voice, "What is it?"

"I don't know," said the sheriff slowly, almost in a whisper. "But it is the most beautiful piece of jewelry I have ever seen."

Uncle Francis added, in a quiet voice, "It is indeed an outstanding work of art. The way the gemstone reflects light is enough to put you in a trance."

"I agree," said Wilmer. "I was in the World War and I have seen medals given to soldiers for bravery and acts of great courage. I have also seen medals given to civilians by governments in war time for service to their country. This one we found in the copper box is similar to a medal given to hospital workers who served in the front lines in Europe. Yes, very similar. This object resembles one of those medals, but is much more beautiful!"

Sam and Howie stood with shoulders slumped and their hands in their pockets. They were very disappointed. They had hoped to see gold or silver coins or perhaps even diamonds in the copper box. An object that resembled a piece of jewelry did not impress them at all. After hearing the comments from the adults they looked at each other and shrugged their shoulders, not knowing what to say.

Finally, Sam spoke first. "Is there anything else in the box?" he asked, hopefully. They had been so intent looking at the beautiful medal no one thought about a further examination of the inside of the box.

"Nope," said the sheriff, after making a final inspection.

He then took a camera off a shelf and proceeded to take several pictures of the medal and the container. When he finished, he said, "After this film is developed, I will make sure the pictures are dated, identified, and entered into our records here at the jail. Then I will give you a copy of each picture for your records."

He continued, "This object may not seem to amount to much lying here on this table, but my instinct tells me that we may have something very valuable here. I am going to put the medal in my office safe now and give you a signed receipt for it. That will keep it protected until it can be identified. You will have a picture of it in a few days so you can research its background."

"Good," said Wilmer, after looking at Howie and Sam. "We'll be back in a few days. Boys, take a good look at the medal. We're going to do some preliminary research to see if we can find out something about it."

The sheriff then wrapped the medal in the soft cloth, put it in the copper box and placed the lid on top. He opened the office safe and placed the box inside. A signed receipt was given to Wilmer.

As they left the jail, Wilmer took out his pocket watch and glanced at the time. "Boys, we're too late again today to go to the library. But, we can come to town after we finish the chores tomorrow morning and go directly there."

All the way home there was constant chatter. The boys became more excited as they discussed the contents of the copper box. Suddenly, from the back seat, Howie yelled out, "I've got it! Do you remember the last mark on the giant horseshoe? It is in the shape of an eight pointed star. I'll bet that final mark on the horseshoe stands for the medal we found in the copper box."

Sam replied excitedly, "Howie, you've done it again. You have just put the final piece of this puzzle in place. That's really good thinking." He reached over and pounded Howie on the back.

Howie's smile reached from ear to ear.

"Yes, he could be right," said Wilmer. "If so, we have a challenge in front of us to research the history of that medal and see if we can identify it."

"Yeah," said Sam, "and, don't forget about the skeleton, and those two strange men who keep showing up to torment us." Howie was quiet but still smiling.

THE ROYAL STAR

CHAPTER 18

THE ROYAL STAR

The next morning the sky was grey and cloudy. The weather forecast in the GrantNews was calling for much needed rain. Millie and Lenora decided to go to Manion with Wilmer, Francis and the boys. They wanted to do some shopping for ladies hats at the R. U. Ready store on the west side of the public square.

After the car was parked on the street, Wilmer, Francis and the boys crossed the street, dodging the electric street car, and walked two city blocks to the public library, a large, three-story building made of Indiana limestone.

Sam leaned over to Howie and whispered, "I never thought we'd end up in a library. This is not nearly as exciting as exploring outdoors."

Howie, with his shirt tail hanging out and his hands in his pockets, just shrugged his shoulders.

Wilmer and the boys entered the library and approached the central area where the card catalogues and files were located. A name plate on the desk gave the librarian's name, a Miss Readmore. She was a tall, thin, attractive woman, wearing a long sleeved, plain black dress with white collar and white buttons down the front. A large piece of jewelry adorned the dress. It was in the shape of a large yellow and green spider with small jewels for eyes. When Howie saw the jewelry, he shuddered. Any object that looked like a spider reminded him of the cobwebs and spiders in the tunnel under the log cabin. Miss Readmore wore wire-rimmed glasses and her hair was neatly snuggled behind her head in a bun.

"May I help you?" she inquired.

"Yes," Wilmer replied. "Do you have any books about medals given to people for bravery in battle or for service to their country in past wars?"

She thought for a moment while looking at some note cards from a file on her desk, and then said, "Yes, we do have a reference book that shows pictures and drawings with descriptions of medals awarded during the last 100 years. I'll get it for you."

When she returned, Wilmer thanked her and took the large, leather-bound volume to a table. They all gathered around to look at the contents.

"I'll turn the pages," said Francis, "and, we'll look for a picture that looks like the medal found in the copper box."

Francis and Wilmer were seated with Sam and Howie looking over their shoulders. They saw many pages of pictures of military medals given in different countries for bravery and service in wartime. Then they came to a section listing medals given for public service. Francis turned the pages slowly. None of the pictures or diagrams seemed to be similar to the medal found in the copper box.

Then Howie shouted, "Hey, look at that one!"

Miss Readmore raised her eyebrows and looked at them over the top of her wire-rimmed glasses and said, "Shush, quiet!"

Their eyes were glued to a drawing of a medal given to hospital workers serving on the battlefields during the Franco-Prussian War fought in the early 1870's. It strongly resembled the medal found in the copper box. The description and the colors fit perfectly.

"Look at it," Sam said quietly. "It's called THE ROYAL STAR."

A description of the medal appeared below the drawing. It was also know as:

THE SPIRIT OF SERVICE MEDAL

Wilmer said, "I think we have found it, but we will wait until we get a copy of the pictures taken by the sheriff in order to be sure. If the photographs match this drawing, I think we may have solved one part of the giant horseshoe mystery."

Wilmer wrote down the name of the reference book and the page number and returned the book to the librarian. They were about to leave when Wilmer had a new idea. He returned to the desk and asked the librarian, "Do you have any information about members of the early churches in this area of Indiana? Some of these people were involved with the Underground Railroad in the early and middle 1800's."

The librarian's eyes lit up. "History is my favorite subject," she said smiling, as she removed her wire-rimmed glasses. "Yes, we have several books with references to churches and the Underground Railroad. These books are on the shelf over there under the clock." She smiled again as she pointed her glasses in the general direction.

"Thank you," responded Wilmer.

He looked at Sam and Howie, and said, "This won't take long. I want to see what information they have about the Underground Railroad."

One of the books had a map showing the routes taken by the runaway slaves on the way north. One of the routes was through Kentucky, then on up to Indianapolis and further north to the state of Michigan.

"That's probably the route that included my Grandpa's log cabin," said Wilmer. "Here are some pictures of homes that were used by the Underground Railroad in Indiana. Some of the homes are still standing and being used today. Here's a picture of a home near Indianapolis that has been turned into a memorial museum. That's amazing!"

"And, here's a list of some last names of people who were involved," said Francis. He ran his finger down the list and stopped on Wilmer's last name. "That could be your Grandpa who built the log cabin, Wilmer."

"Yes," replied Wilmer, "and just think, this information has been here for years and I've not taken the time to come in and read about my own ancestors. Okay, we've done enough today. Let's pick up Millie and Lenora and head back to HayBend."

During the trip back home, the men and boys brought the ladies up to date on their findings at the library.

"Very interesting," said Millie, "but it seems to me the more information we have, the farther away we are from a final solution to the mystery of the giant horseshoe. And, how do those two strange men fit into this mystery?"

* * * *

During the next several days everyone tried to resume normal work on the farm. Wilmer was completing repairs to the barn. Uncle Francis toured the neighborhood selling seed corn. The boys played outside, and the women were busy canning green beans.

After three days had passed, Sheriff Neverfine drove up the lane in his black car and gave Wilmer copies of the photographs taken of the object found in the copper box. He said, "I thought you would like to look at these photos. I received them just today. We will meet in my office the day after tomorrow to review the latest Indiana State Police report."

After the sheriff left, Wilmer and the boys sat down in the farm shop and compared the photos with what they had seen at the library.

"It sure looks like the same medal without the gemstone," said Sam. Howie agreed.

"Yes it does," replied Wilmer. "Although these photos are in black and white, and the drawings in the library are in color, it still seems to be the same. When we go back to the sheriff's office, let's ask him to borrow the library book so we can compare the actual medal with the color drawing."

* * * *

On the appointed day, Wilmer, Francis and the boys made a return trip to the office of Sheriff Neverfine. This time he was expecting them. He had the latest Indiana State Police report, the medal from the copper box, and the photos all out lying on his desk, ready to be examined.

He asked Wilmer and Francis if they would like a cup of coffee. "It's freshly brewed," he said, as he found two mugs in his desk drawer. He filled them with steaming black coffee and handed them to Wilmer and Francis.

"Let me go to my apartment and get two bottles of Jiffy Cola for the two boys."

Sam and Howie smiled. They appreciated the thoughtfulness of the sheriff. Wilmer and Francis sipped the coffee. They licked their lips, raised their eyebrows and looked at each other. Wilmer said, "Jumpin' Lizards, drinking this coffee is like getting a kick from a mule."

When the sheriff returned with the two tall bottles of ice-cold Jiffy Cola, all conversation centered on the object found in the copper container.

"Sheriff, would you ask Miss Readmore at the public library to loan this book to you for a few hours?" asked Wilmer, as he showed him the name of the reference book. "It has a color drawing of a medal similar to the one on your desk."

"Sure," he said, as he took the note and walked out of his office. Shortly, he returned, saying, "Mrs. Stewless will get the book for us right away."

For several minutes they moved around the desk, looking at the photographs and the medal. Again, they were amazed at how the beauty of the green gemstone captured and held their attention. They discussed among themselves the possible name and origin of the gem. Francis suggested it looked like a green garnet. Everyone agreed that it must be a valuable gemstone, and possibly very rare.

Sam and Howie were curious as to the contents of the state police report. Finally, when Sam could not contain himself any longer, he asked, "What about the police report?"

"I'll explain the report later," responded the sheriff.

At that point Mrs. Stewless returned with the reference book from the library. Wilmer turned to the page number he had written down.

"Here it is," he said, and pointed to the Royal Star. "Let's compare this drawing with the medal on the desk." He placed the open book on the desk. Then the sheriff carefully picked up the medal with tongs and placed it next to the drawing.

"A perfect match!" said Wilmer. Francis nodded his head.

The sheriff spoke up. "It looks like we may have identified the medal, The Royal Star, given to hospital workers for their brave service during battles of the Franco-Prussian war in the early 1870's. Someone has added a green gemstone to increase the value of an already attractive medal. I'm going to ask two gemstone experts from Indianapolis to come here to my office. They can identify the gem and place a value on this piece of jewelry."

After a moment, he added, "The question now is…Who is the rightful owner of this beautiful piece of jewelry? I'm going to put it back in my office safe until we find that person. I'll also talk to the reporter for the GrantNews so he can make the public aware of our progress in this case. Perhaps that news will bring someone forward with information. We will need to have another meeting in about a week here in my office."

* * * *

During the next several days the routine at HayBend returned to normal. Sam and Howie, however, were as tense as ever, thinking about the skeleton, the horseshoe, the medal and the two strange men.

In three days the GrantNews printed a two-column story telling about the progress made in solving the case of the skeleton and the giant horseshoe found in the tunnel under the log cabin on Grandpa George's property. The headline read:

THE MYSTERY OF THE

GIANT HORSESHOE!!

The reporter told about Sam and Howie solving the meaning of the markings on the giant horseshoe. He also wrote about the boys locating the copper container in the fireplace wall, and finding inside an object that resembled a medal called The Royal Star. Then the reporter told about the history of the Royal Star and why it was an important medal. An appeal went out to the public for information leading to the rightful owner. The gemstone was not mentioned.

Sam finished reading the news article. He asked his dad, "Why didn't the reporter tell about the gemstone?"

"The sheriff doesn't want a lot of false information coming into his office. There are people who might claim the medal just to get the gemstone."

"Yeah," agreed Sam, "no wonder those two strangers have been threatening us! But how did they know something valuable might be hidden in the log cabin?"

CHAPTER 19

SLY AND SLICK IN JAIL

The day after the news story appeared, Sheriff Neverfine drove out to Wilmer and Millie's farmstead. He got out of his shiny, black Ford and was starting to walk toward the house when Wilmer, emerging from the farm shop, saw him.

"Hi, sheriff, we didn't expect you out today."

"I have some important news I wanted to share with you regarding the Royal Star. Are the boys around? I want them to hear this information, too."

"Yes, they're out in the barn with Sam's air rifle trying to scare the pigeons."

He started to call for them when they came running. "We saw the sheriff's black car," said Sam, out of breath. He leaned the BB gun against a maple tree.

"Good," said the sheriff. "Let's sit in the car here in the shade with the doors open so we can be a little cooler."

He opened all four doors and they all piled in, anxious to hear what the sheriff had to say.

"I think we may have a break in this case," he began. "The two strangers who were accused of trespassing on your neighbor's property several days ago were arrested yesterday. They were trying to steal gasoline from the same farmer.

The neighbor who lives across the road was alert. He noticed the same black car parked beside the road. He drove to my office and informed me about the car and described it. When I arrived at the scene the man with red hair was walking very fast toward their car from your neighbor's garage carrying two gallon cans full of gasoline. The dark haired man was waiting in the car with the motor running. I arrested them both for trespassing and theft, fingerprinted them and booked them in our jail. While they were in jail, the Indiana State Police ran routine checks of their fingerprints to see if they were wanted for any other crimes."

Howie and Sam looked at their fingers and then at each other. "Are my fingerprints different from Howie's?" asked Sam.

"Indeed they are," assured the sheriff.

Sheriff Neverfine continued, "Based on their fingerprints, we learned the two men are from Kentucky. They have been wanted for years by the Kentucky State Police for break-in and robbery at several homes. One police report contains a list of items stolen. It seems one of the items stolen from a home was a medal described to be similar to the one in my office safe."

"Wow!" said Howie.

"Jumpin' Lizards!" commented Wilmer.

"I wanted you to know about this latest development. These men are now behind bars, so you won't need to have any fear for your safety as far as they are concerned. Two Kentucky state policemen are coming to my jail tomorrow and we are going to interview these men. Please come to my office in two days. Maybe we can put another piece of this puzzle together."

"We'll be there," said Sam, Howie, and Wilmer at the same time.

* * * *

On the morning of the second day, Wilmer, Francis, Sam and Howie drove to Manion and walked directly to the sheriff's office. After the usual greetings, the sheriff spoke. "First, I want to take all of you up to the floor where the prisoners are in their cells. We'll see if Sam and Howie can identify any of the men as the two persons they saw at the log cabin." Now, Sam and Howie became very nervous. They felt the hair on the backs of their necks begin to rise. They didn't want to confront the two men again.

"We're going to walk along the entire row of cells," said the sheriff. "Don't react or point to any of the prisoners. Take a good look at all the men. Don't say a word until we are back in my office. Is that clear?"

"Yes…s…s," stammered both Howie and Sam.

They followed the sheriff up to the second floor and slowly walked in front of the cells holding the prisoners. Some of the men were resting on their bunks and others were standing behind the bars with their arms hanging outside. When the two men in cell number two saw Sam and Howie coming, they turned their backs and faced the far wall. The boys could see that one man had long red hair and the other had dark hair. Seeing the men again made them tremble with fear.

When they returned to the sheriff's office he asked the boys, "Well, did you recognize anyone?"

"Y…Yeah," said Sam, his fear calming, "the two men in cell number two. One has red hair and the other has dark hair. They are the men who were in the log cabin. I could recognize them from the backs of their heads."

"Yeah," said Howie, "they match the body shapes of the men we saw at the cabin. One was thinner and the other was stronger looking."

"Okay," replied the sheriff. "Now I'm going to tell you what we have learned from interviewing these two men. Have a seat. This may take a while."

They all sat down on the wooden office chairs and leaned forward, expecting the sheriff to say something important.

"The man with dark hair goes by the name of Sly. The man with red hair has the nickname Slick. Two Kentucky state policemen and I spent many hours questioning these two men. Are you ready for a long session?"

"Yeah," replied the group. Sam and Howie sat on the edges of their chairs, eager to hear the rest of the story.

CHAPTER 20

PUFF: THE REST OF THE STORY

The sheriff began. "We offered to drop the charges of trespassing and theft of the gasoline here in Indiana. In turn, the State of Kentucky will charge them with several counts of burglary. This procedure could result in less jail time for Sly and Slick, but it gave us a more complete picture of their past activities in Kentucky and Indiana. In exchange for dropping the charges here in Indiana, they agreed to tell us the complete story of their criminal history, going back at least 15 years. Their lawyer agreed to this plan.

In the beginning there were three men who were involved in a series of burglaries in Kentucky. These crimes included home break-ins over a number of years. About 12 years ago, the three were just ahead of the Kentucky State Police when they crossed the state line to Indiana. The three decided to separate in Indiana, one going his own way, and Sly and Slick, who are in jail here, staying together."

Continuing, the sheriff said, "Before the three men separated, they divided the items taken from the homes during the burglaries. The man who separated from the other two was called Puff. This nickname came about because he always puffed out his chest when he was younger so he would appear larger and manlier. He took as his share only a copper container about 10 inches long, 5 inches wide and 5 inches high. He said that Sly and Slick could have everything else.

It seems that Puff had told Sly and Slick about the history of the Underground Railroad in Indiana and some of the homes involved. As a child he had listened to his parents and other relatives, who were church members, talk about how their ancestors helped runaway slaves escape to Canada. They told him about the places along the route where the slaves were hidden, including the log cabin on your Grandpa George's farm with the underground tunnel."

Sam and Howie, leaning forward, were all ears as they sat silently, trying to keep track of the events the sheriff was explaining.

Sheriff Neverfine, shifting in his chair, added, "Puff also heard his aunt talk about a medal her mother had received for bravery as a nurse during the Franco-Prussian war. She kept the medal, wrapped in a soft cloth, in a copper container and, on occasion, showed it to guests. The aunt had a jeweler add a gemstone to the medal to convert it into a piece of jewelry. The gemstone had been given to her by an admirer who had traveled in Russia. This is the reason Puff wanted the copper container. He told Sly and Slick they could have the rest of the stolen items. He added that the medal should be his since it had belonged to his distant relative.

When Puff was in his teens, he worked for his neighbors, one being a blacksmith. However, he spent most of his time with two neighbor boys, Sly and Slick, who were constantly in trouble with the law. A few years later, the men teamed up and started breaking into houses and stealing jewelry and other items of value. They would then sell the items and divide the money."

"Rascals!" muttered Howie.

At that point Sheriff Neverfine said, "I think we all need a short break. Let's walk over to my apartment and get some Jiffy Cola out of the refrigerator and then we'll come back and continue this exciting story."

When they returned to the sheriff's office, each with a 12 ounce bottle of bubbly, ice-cold Jiffy Cola, they were ready to hear the sheriff continue.

"One night, the three thieves broke into the home of Puff's aunt and stole the copper container with the medal along with other jewelry. By now, the Kentucky State Police were on their trail. They fled north toward Indiana. As they crossed the state line they decided to divide the loot and separate.

Puff told them he was headed for the log cabin on your property.

He knew he could hide from the police in the tunnel under the cabin. He told Sly and Slick that if the police followed him to the log cabin he would find a hiding place for the copper container. They agreed to meet in 30 days at Eatmore's Greasy Plate Diner on route 40 east of Indianapolis to plan more robberies.

A few days later, Sly and Slick read in a newspaper that the Indiana State Police had trailed a robbery suspect to a farm in Grantor County but found no one and the trail went cold. Sly and Slick knew then Puff had devised a plan for hiding the medal, probably in the log cabin. They also knew that Puff had hid in the tunnel to escape the police.

The story really gets exciting now," continued the sheriff, as he inhaled, smiled and leaned back in his chair. He took a big swig of Jiffy Cola, burped, and placed the empty bottle on his desk.

"At the end of 30 days the three met at Eatmore's Greasy Plate Diner to plan future break-ins. Puff told Sly and Slick he had hidden in the tunnel under the log cabin. He said after the police left, he crawled back to the cabin, came up through the trap door and put his plan to work. He decided to hide the copper box in the cabin.

He then told them he had devised several clues to show where the copper container was hidden. He planned to take the clues with him and return in the future. The clues would remind him as to the location of the container. Also, in the future, if he needed money, he could sell the clues to another person. Puff told Sly and Slick he had marked the clues on a piece of metal shaped like a horseshoe."

Sam and Howie squirmed in their chairs. They were beginning to understand why Sly and Slick were so interested in stealing the giant horseshoe.

The sheriff looked at his notes taken during his interview with Sly and Slick, then, after burping again, he continued, "Puff decided to use his knowledge of blacksmithing to mark the clues on the metal. He stole some hard coal from one of your neighbors and built a hot fire in the cabin fireplace. He made a large horseshoe-shaped object out of a flat piece of metal he found in the barn on your Grandpa George's farm. With a chisel he made the markings on the horseshoe as clues to the location of the copper container."

The sheriff leaned forward and looked at Sam and Howie. "Now the story gets even more interesting!"

Sam and Howie were all ears. They now realized that the sheriff was also a great story teller. They drained their bottles of Jiffy Cola and sat very still. The sheriff had their full attention.

"While the three thieves were at the diner, two local sheriffs' deputies walked in and sat at the next table. As the deputies ate their meals, they talked about being hot on the trail of three robbery suspects from Kentucky. After hearing the deputy's talk, Puff, Sly and Slick left Eatmore's Greasy Plate Diner in a hurry and decided to split up and go into hiding.

Puff told Sly and Slick he was going back to the log cabin. The other two said they were going to return to Kentucky. They never saw or heard from Puff again."

The sheriff continued, with enthusiasm, "Indiana State Police records show one of their troopers and a local Grantor County sheriff's deputy arrived at the log cabin again on a tip Puff had returned to the area. Sly and Slick did not admit to me they were the ones who gave the police the tip. However, it is possible they wanted Puff behind bars so they could find the copper container and claim the medal.

Since Puff told Sly and Slick he was going to the log cabin, and since he was never heard from again, the state police believe he took the horseshoe with him as he hid from the police in the tunnel. We believe Puff died at that time while in the tunnel… possibly of a rattlesnake bite."

"I'll be plague gone!" said Francis. "He died of a snake bite!"

"Jumpin' Lizards!" said Wilmer. "A rattlesnake bite. I wouldn't have guessed it."

"Wow!" said Howie, with alarm, "a snake bite! Sam and I saw a big black snake in the tunnel. We could have died from a snake bite."

"The black snake is not poisonous, Howie," reminded Wilmer.

"Oh, okay," replied Howie, with relief.

The sheriff then picked up the most recent state police report from his desk. "The second Indiana State Police report indicates the poison that caused death was from snake venom. When their laboratory people examined the skeleton more closely, they found possible snake fang marks on one of the lower leg bones. That discovery led to the idea of a snake bite. They used dental records to prove the skeleton belongs to Puff.

Sly and Slick continued robbing and stealing over the years. This summer they decided to try again to find the copper container. They came to the log cabin on the farm. When they saw Sam and Howie with the giant horseshoe, they knew it was the key to the hiding place.

They remembered our Puff was a blacksmith's helper at one time, and he had marked clues on a piece of metal shaped like a horseshoe. They did not know that Puff had chiseled two holes in the fireplace wall to fit the bent ends of the giant horseshoe. Also, Sly and Slick did not know that the location of the horseshoe on the fireplace wall indicated how the clues would lead to the copper container that was hidden back of a particular stone.

That is the reason they took the horseshoe from the fireplace wall. They heard the boys discuss the markings and their meanings. They were planning to come back to the cabin with the giant horseshoe. Then, they were going to put it up on the fireplace wall and try to find the container with the medal. And that, folks, is the rest of the story," said the sheriff, with a smile of satisfaction. He gathered up his papers and placed them in a neat pile. "Now we know the solution to the mystery of the giant horseshoe."

"Wow!" said both boys in unison, as they slapped each other on the back.

"Before you leave, I have arranged for the newspaper reporter from the GrantNews to come to my office and take some photographs of Sam and Howie. He will want to talk to you boys again. He will write another story about how you two helped to solve the mystery of the giant horseshoe found in the tunnel under the log cabin on your grandfather's farm.

Oh, by the way, when we searched the black car driven by Sly and Slick, we found the giant horseshoe. The police will not need it for evidence at the trial for Sly and Slick. They will be charged with burglary in Kentucky. I thought you boys might like to have it," he said, as he handed it to Sam and Howie.

"Thanks, sheriff," said Sam and Howie together, as they proudly accepted the horseshoe.

Wilmer, Francis, Howie and Sam all piled into the car for the trip home. Everyone was smiling and happy that the mystery of the giant horseshoe had been solved. Sam and Howie slapped each other on the back. They were proud they played an important part in solving the mystery.

Wilmer drove up the long lane and parked near the rear porch of the house. Sam and Howie bounded out of the car and ran inside anxious to share their good news with Millie and Lenora. Soon everyone was gathered in the kitchen, smiling and chattering about the solution to the mystery. Indeed, it had been an eventful day.

* * * *

Two days later the daughter of the aunt who had owned the Royal Star contacted Sheriff Neverfine. She had read the story about the Royal Star in the GrantNews. She provided photographs and a copy of her aunt's will as proof of ownership. She said she was going to donate The Royal Star medal with gemstone to the Indiana State Museum of History. She wanted to do this to honor the role of nurses and all hospital workers on and off the battlefields of past wars.

CHAPTER 21

THE MYSTERY SOLVED

Sheriff Neverfine made a final trip out to The HayBend Farm. Sam's sister, Mary, had returned from visiting with her friend Judy. As the sheriff drove up to the house, Wilmer, Millie, Francis, Lenora, Sam, Howie and Mary all came out to greet him. Sam was carrying his B B gun and the giant horseshoe. They gathered around his shiny, black car. He turned off the engine and rolled down his window. He was wearing a crisp, tan uniform that provided an appropriate background for the sheriff's badge on his chest and the chevron stripes on his sleeves. He was smiling as he took off his hat and placed it on the seat beside him.

"Hi, everyone, I wanted to tell you what has happened since our last discussion a few days ago in my office." They could tell he was in a good mood.

"The daughter of the aunt who owned the Royal Star medal came to my office yesterday and showed me proof she is the rightful owner. She had read about The Royal Star in the GrantNews. She is going to donate the medal and gemstone to the Indiana State Museum of History. The museum has a special room for displaying articles and information related to the wars and battles fought on foreign soil.

Now, are you folks ready for some more amazing information?"

All leaned forward and listened intently.

"I have received estimates of value for The Royal Star and the gemstone. Both of the gemologists from Indianapolis who appraised the medal identified the gemstone as a Demantoid, one of the most brilliant gems that exist. The Demantoid was discovered in Russia in

1868. The surface of the gem splits the light into all the colors of the rainbow when properly cut."

The sheriff continued, his voice rising, "Also, the Demantoid on this medal contains the 'horsetail inclusion,' which appears as golden brown threads. This rarity makes it extremely valuable. The gemologists said the value of this medal with gemstone cannot be estimated. It is very rare and cannot be replaced. Two state policemen are coming to my office soon to take it and deliver it to the museum where it will be placed in a secure glass display case."

Everyone shuffled their shoes in the gravel, smiled and looked at each other with amazement and satisfaction.

Finally, Wilmer spoke up, "I can speak for all of us, sheriff. We greatly appreciate your help in solving the mystery of the giant horseshoe, as Sam and Howie call it."

"Well, without the help from these two boys, this case would still be a mystery," replied the sheriff, as he reached out and gave Sam and Howie a pat on the shoulder.

Sam and Howie, with hands in their pockets, looked down at their shoes, not knowing how to accept the compliment. With big grins on their faces, they finally looked up at Sheriff Neverfine as a family friend. As their eyes met, all three knew they were now "comrades in arms."

Sheriff Neverfine broke the silence. "Since the Indiana State Police think Puff died of a poisonous snake bite, I don't have an unsolved murder on my hands. And friends, we now have two burglary suspects, Sly and Slick, in a Kentucky jail, awaiting trial."

He added, "I cannot thank all of you enough, especially Sam and Howie. You two boys continued to press on with the search for a solution to this mystery even when we adults thought there was no mystery. You not only solved the mystery of the giant horseshoe, but your findings led to the recovery of the valuable Royal Star medal and gemstone that had been missing for years. Now, thousands of people will be able to enjoy this outstanding and valuable medal with gemstone as they visit the Indiana State Museum of History.

Well, I must go now. Duty calls," he said, as he placed his hat on his head and stepped on the starter button. The Ford's V-8 engine responded with a roar, and then quieted to a pleasant humming noise. Wilmer and Millie quietly closed the doors to the car and everyone stepped back.

As the black police car started to roll down the gravel lane, Sheriff Neverfine shouted out the open window, "Sam and Howie, you have helped me to have a very pleasant and rewarding summer! Thank you. And best wishes to you all."

He waved his hand out the car window. Then his foot found the gas pedal and the shiny black Ford, with the siren on the front fender, the spotlight and the whitewall tires was quickly lost in the dust of the long gravel lane.

* * * *

The next day Francis, Lenora and Howie packed their suitcases and were ready to depart HayBend. Wilmer had walked to the mailbox to pick up the morning mail. When he returned, he was reading the front page of the GrantNews.

"Look here," he shouted, "Sam and Howie are on the front page again!" A large headline in bold print read:

TWO LOCAL LADS SOLVE

GIANT HORSESHOE MYSTERY!!

There it was, a large picture of Sam in his bib overalls and Howie with his shirt tail hanging out. They were grinning and holding the giant horseshoe between them. Along with the picture there was a complete story about how they helped solve the mystery of the giant horseshoe. Three columns of print described how the boys had worked on the case to determine the meaning of each clue as it appeared on the side of the horseshoe.

Included was a picture and history of the Royal Star with gemstone. The reporter explained the medal had been crafted into a stunning piece of jewelry by adding the Demantoid gemstone with the horsetail inclusion. The appraisal of the medal and gemstone was mentioned.

A paragraph praised the owner of The Royal Star for donating it to the Indiana State Museum of History. The story concluded with a small picture of Sly and Slick, indicating they were residing in a Kentucky jail, awaiting trial. The skeleton of Puff was being buried in a family cemetery in Kentucky.

After everyone had read the latest news, Uncle Francis put the suitcases in the trunk of the green Chevrolet and slammed the lid. Lenora, in an unusual gesture of affection, gave Millie, Mary and Sam a hug. Wilmer and Francis shook hands without comment. Sam and Howie just stood and looked at each other. Howie had told Sam he could have the giant horseshoe to hang in his room as a reminder of their exciting times together.

Finally, Uncle Francis and his family got into the car and closed the doors. They waved their arms out of the open windows. As they were slowly pulling away from the HayBend farmstead, Sam ran behind the moving car and hollered, "Howie, I am already planning for your next visit. We are going to explore that vacant house across the road. You remember the house our great grandpa and grandma moved into when they outgrew the log cabin!"

Sam could see Howie's head bobbing up and down in agreement. His smiling face was framed by the rear window of the green Chevrolet as it moved slowly down the gravel lane.

Then, Wilmer, Millie, Mary and Sam turned and walked slowly toward the house. It seemed everyone, including Millie, did not want this pleasant visit to end.

Sam, however, was already lost in his thoughts. With giant horseshoe in one hand and his BB gun in the other hand, his mind was racing ahead as he was planning their next discovery adventure.

"Howie and I will make another wild and important discovery in that vacant house across the road when he returns on his next visit," he said to himself. "I just feel it in my bones." Then he shivered as the thought of bones reminded him of Puff's skeleton, one of the main characters in the giant horseshoe mystery.

ABOUT THE AUTHOR

George S. Haines grew up on a farm in North Central Indiana during the 1930's and 1940's. He is aware of the pleasures and problems that people experienced in rural areas during that time period. He knows first hand the excitement that young boys enjoyed by having relatives and friends visit the farm bringing a change of pace to the daily routine of life in the country.

He graduated from Purdue University with B.S. and M.S. degrees. His doctorate was earned at George Peabody College for Teachers. He has taught students from the seventh grade through adults. At Taylor University, Upland, Indiana, he was professor of education and Director of Teacher Education during a 17 year tenure. He lives in Ft. Myers, Florida.

ABOUT THE ARTIST

Betty Wedeles is a talented artist who has studied under Gene Melton of the University of Southern California. She has taught beginning and advanced art classes for 27 years. She has judged at art shows and taught workshops. Her knowledge of color, harmony, value, measurement and composition is conveyed to her students. She is also involved in wood carving, clay sculpture and china painting. Many of her artistic endeavors reflect her respect for wildlife and its habitat. Mrs. Wedeles lives in Ft. Myers, Florida.

LaVergne, TN USA
21 October 2010
201802LV00003B/42/P